THE WORLD JONES MADE

Also by Philip K. Dick

Solar Lottery (1955)
The Man Who Japed (1956)
Eye in the Sky (1957)
The Cosmic Puppets (1957)
Dr. Futurity (1959)
Time Out of Joint (1959)
Vulcan's Hammer (1960)
The Man in the High Castle (1962)
The Game-Players of Titan (1963)
The Penultimate Truth (1964)
The Simulacra (1964)
Martian Time-Slip (1964)
Clans of the Alphane Moon (1964)
The Three Stigmata of Palmer
   Eldritch (1965)
Dr. Bloodmoney, or How We Got
   Along After the Bomb (1965)
Cantata-140 (The Crack in Space)
   (1966)
Now Wait for Last Year (1966)
The Ganymede Takeover (with
   Ray F. Nelson) (1967)
The Zap Gun (1967)
Counter-Clock World (1967)
Do Androids Dream of Electric
   Sheep? (1968)
Galactic Pot-Healer (1969)
Ubik (1969)
Our Friends from Frolix 8 (1970)
A Maze of Death (1970)
We Can Build You (1972)
Flow My Tears, The Policeman
   Said (1974)
Confessions of a Crap Artist (1975)

Deus Irae (with Roger Zelazny)
   (1976)
A Scanner Darkly (1977)
The Divine Invasion (1981)
Valis (1981)
The Transmigration of Timothy
   Archer (1982)
Lies, Inc (1984)
The Man Whose Teeth Were All
   Exactly Alike (1984)
Puttering About in a Small Land
   (1985)
In Milton Lumky Territory (1985)
Radio Free Albemuth (1985)
Humpty Dumpty in Oakland (1986)
Mary and the Giant (1987)
The Broken Bubble (1988)

SHORT STORY COLLECTIONS

The Variable Man (1957)
A Handful of Darkness (1966)
The Turning Wheel (1977)
The Best of Philip K. Dick (1977)
The Golden Man (1980)
Minority Report (2002)

THE COLLECTED STORIES OF
PHILIP K. DICK

1. Beyond Lies the Wub (1987)
2. Second Variety (1987)
3. The Father Thing (1987)
4. The Days of Perky Pat (1987)
5. We Can Remember It For You
   Wholesale (1987)

THE WORLD JONES MADE

Philip K. Dick

Copyright © Philip K. Dick 1956
All rights reserved

First published in Great Britain in this edition in 2003 by

Gollancz
An imprint of the Orion Publishing Group
Orion House, 5 Upper St Martin's Lane,
London WC2H 9EA

A CIP catalogue record for this book
is available from the British Library

ISBN 0 575 07457 4

Printed in Great Britain by
Clays Ltd, St Ives plc

To Eph Konigsburg
who talked fast
and talked very well

THE WORLD JONES MADE

1

The temperature of the Refuge varied from 99 degrees Fahrenheit to 101 degrees Fahrenheit. Steam lay perenially in the air, drifting and billowing sluggishly. Geysers of hot water spurted, and the "ground" was a shifting surface of warm slime, compounded from water, dissolved minerals, and fungoid pulp. The remains of lichens and protozoa colored and thickened the scum of moisture that dripped everywhere, over the wet rocks and sponge-like shrubbery, the various utilitarian installations. A careful backdrop had been painted, a long plateau rising from a heavy ocean.

Beyond doubt, the Refuge was modelled after the womb. The semblance couldn't be denied—and nobody *had* denied it.

Bending down, Louis moodily picked up a pale green fungus growing near his feet and broke it apart. Under its moist organic skin was a mesh of man-made plastic; the fungus was artificial.

"We could be worse off," Frank said, watching him hurl the fungus away. "We might have to pay for all this. It must have cost Fedgov billions of dollars to set up this place."

"Stage scenery," Louis said bitterly. "What for? Why were we born this way?"

Grinning, Frank said: "We're superior mutants, remember? Isn't that what we decided years ago?" He pointed at the world visible beyond the wall of the Refuge. "We're too pure for that."

Outside lay San Francisco, the nocturnal city half-asleep in its blanket of chill fog. Occasional cars crept here and there; pockets of commuters emerged like complicated segmented worms from underground monorail terminals. Infrequent office light glowed sparsely . . . Louis turned his back on the sight. It hurt too much to see it, to know that he was in here, trapped, caught within the closed circle of the group. To realize that nothing existed for them but the sitting and staring, the empty years of the Refuge.

"There must be a purpose," he said. "A reason for us."

Frank shrugged fatalistically. "War-time sports, generated by radiation pools. Damage to the genes. An accident . . . like Jones."

"But they're keeping us alive," Irma said, from behind them. "All these years, maintaining us, caring for us. They must get something out of it. They must have something in mind."

"Destiny?" Frank asked mockingly. "Our cosmic goal?"

The Refuge was a murky, steamy bowl that imprisoned the seven of them. Its atmosphere was a mixture of ammonia, oxygen, freon, and traces of methane, heavily laden with water vapor, lacking carbon dioxide. The Refuge had been constructed twenty-five years ago, in 1977, and the older members of the group had memories of a prior life in separate mechanical incubators. The original workmanship had been superior, and from time to time improvements were made. Normal human workmen, protected by sealed suits, periodically entered the Refuge, dragging their maintenance equipment after them. Usually it was the mobile fauna that went out of order and needed repairs.

"If they had a purpose for us," Frank said, "they'd tell us." He, personally, trusted the Fedgov authorities who operated the Refuge. "Doctor Rafferty would tell us; you know that."

"I'm not so sure," Irma said.

"My God," Frank said angrily, "they're not our enemies. If they wanted to, they could wipe us out in a second—and they haven't, have they? They could let the Youth League in here at us."

"They have no right to keep us in here," Louis protested.

Frank sighed. "If we went out there," he said carefully, as if he were speaking to children, "we'd die." At the upper rim of the transparent wall was a pressure vent, a series of safety valves. A dull miasma of acrid gasses trickled in, mixing with the familiar dampness of their own air. "Smell that?" Frank demanded. "That's what it's like outside. Harsh and freezing and lethal."

"Did it ever occur to you," Louis asked, "that maybe that stuff leaking in is a deliberate fake?"

"It occurs to all of us," Frank said. "Every couple of years. We get in our paranoia stage and we start planning to break out. Only we don't have to break out; all we have to do is walk out. Nobody ever stopped us. We're free to leave this steamed-up bowl, except for one fact: *we can't survive out there. We're just not strong enough.*"

By the transparent wall, a hundred feet away, stood the remaining four members of the group. Frank's voice carried to them, a hollow and distorted sound. Garry, the youngest of the group, glanced up. He listened for a moment, but no further words were audible.

"Okay," Vivian said impatiently. "Let's go."

Garry nodded. "Goodbye womb," he muttered. Reaching

up, he pressed the red button that would bring Doctor
Rafferty.

Doctor Rafferty said: "Our small friends get somewhat excited, once in awhile. They've decided they can lick any man
in the house." He led Cussick to the upramp. "This will be
interesting . . . your first time. Don't be surprised; it may be
a shock. They're quite different from us, physiologically
speaking."

At the eleventh floor the first elements of the Refuge were
visible, the elaborate pumps that maintained its temperature
and atmosphere. Doctors instead of police were visible, white
uniforms instead of brown. On the fourteenth floor Rafferty
stepped from the rising ramp, and Cussick followed.

"They're ringing for you," a doctor said to Rafferty.
"They're highly disturbed, these days."

"Thanks." To Cussick, Rafferty said: "You can watch on
that screen. I don't want them to see you. They shouldn't be
aware of the police guard."

A section of wall retired. Beyond it was the swirling blue-
green landscape of the Refuge. Cussick watched as Doctor
Rafferty strode through the lock and into the artificial world
beyond. Immediately the tall figure was surrounded by seven
curious parodies, gnomish miniatures both male and female.
The seven of them were agitated, and their frail, bird-cage
chests rose and fell with emotion. Crying shrilly, excitedly,
they began to explain and gesture.

"What is it?" Rafferty interrupted. In the sweltering steam
of the Refuge he was gasping for breath; perspiration dripped
from his reddening face.

"We want to leave here," a female piped.

"And we're walking," another announced, a male. "We've
decided—you can't keep us shut up in here. We have rights."

For an interval Rafferty discussed the situation with them;
then, abruptly, he turned and made his way back through

the lock. "That's my limit," he murmured to Cussick, mopping his forehead. "I can tolerate three minutes in there, and then the ammonia goes to work."

"You're going to let them try it?" Cussick asked.

"Activate the Van," Rafferty said to his technicians. "Have it ready to pick them up as they drop." To Cussick he explained: "The Van is an iron lung for them. There won't be too much risk; they're fragile, but we'll be ready to gather them up before damage is done."

Not all the mutants were leaving the Refuge. Four hesitant figures were picking their way along the passage that led to the elevator. Behind them, their three companions remained in the safety of the entrance, huddled together in a group.

"Those three are more realistic," Doctor Rafferty said. "And older. The slightly heavier one, the dark-haired one who looks the most human, is Frank. It's the younger ones who give us the trouble. I'll put them through a gradational series of stages to acclimatize their overly-vulnerable systems—so they won't suffocate or die of heart stoppage." Worriedly, he went on: "What I want you to do is clear the streets. I don't want anybody to see them; it's late and there won't be many people out, but just in case . . ."

"I'll phone Secpol," Cussick agreed.

"How soon can it be done?"

"A few minutes. The weapons-police are already mobile, because of Jones and the mobs."

Relieved, Rafferty hurried off, and Cussick began searching for a Security police phone. He found it, got in touch with the San Francisco office, and gave his instructions. While he kept the phone circuit open, the airborne police teams began collecting around the Refuge building. He stayed in direct touch until the street-blocks had been erected, and then he left the phone to look for Rafferty.

By elevator the four mutants had descended to the street level. Staggering, groping numbly, they followed Doctor Rafferty across the lobby, toward the wide doors that led to the street.

No pedestrians or cars were in sight, Cussick observed; the police had successfully cleared everybody away. At the corner one gloomy shape broke the expanse of gray; the Van was parked, its motor running, ready to follow.

"There they go," a doctor said, standing beside Cussick. "I hope Rafferty knows what he's doing." He pointed. "The almost-pretty one is Vivian. She's the youngest female. The boy is Garry—very bright, very unstable. That is Dieter, and his companion is Louis. There's an eighth, a baby, still in the incubator. They haven't as yet been told."

The four diminutive figures were visibly suffering. Half-conscious, two of them in convulsions, they crept wretchedly down the steps, trying to stay on their feet. They did not get far. Garry was the first to go down; he tottered for a moment on the last step and then pitched face-forward onto the cement. His small body quivering, he tried to crawl forward; sightlessly, the others stumbled along the sidewalk, unaware of the prone shape among them, too far gone themselves even to register its existence.

"Well," Dieter gasped, "we're outside."

"We—made it," Vivian agreed. Sinking wearily down she rested against the side of the building. A moment later Dieter lay sprawled beside her, eyes shut, mouth slack, struggling weakly to get to his feet. And presently Louis slid down beside them.

Chagrined, dazed by the suddenness of their collapse, the four of them lay huddled feebly against the gray pavement, trying to breathe, trying to stay alive. None of them made any attempt to move; the purpose of their ordeal was forgotten. Panting, struggling to hold onto consciousness, they gazed sightlessly at the upright figure of Doctor Rafferty.

Rafferty had halted, hands in his overcoat pockets. "It's up to you," he said stonily. "You want to go on?"

None of them answered; none of them even heard him.

"Your systems won't take the natural air," Rafferty continued. "Or the temperature. Or the food. Or anything." He glanced at Cussick, an expression of pain on his face, an acute reflection of suffering that startled the Security official. "So let's give up," he said harshly. "Let's call the Van and go back."

Vivian nodded faintly; her lips moved, but there was no sound.

Turning, Rafferty curtly signalled. The Van rolled instantly up; robot equipment dropped to the pavement and scuttled up to the four collapsed figures. In a moment they were being lifted into the Van's locks. The expedition had failed; it was over. Cussick had had his view of them. He had seen their struggle and their defeat.

For a time he and Doctor Rafferty stood on the cold night sidewalk without speaking, each involved in his own thoughts. Finally Rafferty stirred. "Thanks for clearing the streets," he murmured.

"I'm glad I had time," Cussick answered. "It might have been bad . . . some of Jones' Youth League Patrols are roaming around."

"The eternal Jones. We really don't have a chance."

"Let's be like these four we just saw; let's keep trying."

"But it's true."

"It's true," Cussick agreed. "Just as it's true your mutants can't breathe out here. But we set up roadblocks anyhow; we cleared the streets and hoped to hell we pushed them back this one time."

"Have you ever seen Jones?"

"Several times," Cussick said. "I met him face to face, back in the days before he had an organization, before anybody had heard of him."

"When he was a minister," Rafferty reflected. "With a church."

"Before that," Cussick said, thinking back. It seemed impossible that there had been a time before Jones, a time when there had been no need of clearing the streets. When there had been no gray-uniformed shapes roaming the streets, collecting in mobs. The crash of breaking glass, the furious crackling of fire . . .

"What was he doing then?" Rafferty asked.

"He was in a carnival," Cussick said.

2

He was twenty-six years old when he first met Jones. It was April 4, 1995. He always remembered that day; the spring air was cool and full of the smell of new growth. The war had ended the year before.

Ahead of him spread out a long descending slope. Houses were perched here and there, mostly privately-constructed shelters, temporary and flimsy. Crude streets, working-class people wandering . . . a typical rural region that had survived, remote from industrial centers. Normally there would be the hum of activity: plows and forges and crude manufacturing processes. But today a quiet hung over the community. Most able-bodied adults, and all of the children, had trudged off to the carnival.

The ground was soft and moist under his shoes. Cussick strode eagerly along, because he, too, was going to the carnival. He had a job.

Jobs were scarce; he was glad to get it. Like other young men intellectually sympathetic to Hoff's Relativism, he had applied for the government service. Fedgov's apparatus offered a chance to become involved in the task of Reconstruction; as he was earning a salary—paid in stable silver—he was helping mankind.

In those days he had been idealistic.

Specifically, he had been assigned to the Interior Department. At the Baltimore Antipol center he had taken political training and then approached Secpol: the Security arm. But the task of suppressing extremist political and religious sentiment had, in 1995, seemed merely bureaucratic. Nobody took it seriously; with worldwide food rationing, the panic was over. Everybody could be sure of basic subsistence. Wartime fanaticism had dwindled out of existence as rational control regained its pre-inflation position.

Before him, spread out like a sheet of tin, the carnival sat assembled. Ten metal buildings, displaying bright neon signs, were the main structures. A central lane led to the hub: a cone within which seats had been erected. There, the basic acts would take place.

Already, he could see the first familiar spectacle. Pushing ahead, Cussick made his way among the densely-packed mass of people. The odor of sweat and tobacco rose around him, an exciting smell. Sliding past a family of grimy field laborers, he reached the railing of the first freak exhibit, and gazed up.

The war, with its hard radiation and elaborate diseases, had produced countless sports, oddities, freaks. Here, in this one minor carnival, a vast variety had been collected.

Directly above him sat a multi-man, a tangled mass of flesh and organs. Heads, arms, legs, wobbled dully; the creature was feeble-minded and helpless. Fortunately, his offspring would be normal; the multi-organisms were not true mutants.

"Golly," a portly, curly-headed citizen behind him said, horrified. "Isn't that awful?"

Another man, lean and tall, casually remarked: "Saw a lot of them in the war. We burned a barnful of them, a sort of colony."

The portly man blinked, bit deep into his candied apple, and moved away from the war veteran. Leading his wife and three children, he meandered up beside Cussick.

"Horrible, isn't it?" he muttered. "All these monsters."

"Sort of," Cussick admitted.

"I don't know why I come to these things." The portly man indicated his wife and children, all of them stonily gobbling up their popcorn and spun-sugar candy. "They like to come. Women and kids go in for this stuff."

Cussick said: "Under Relativism we have to let them live."

"Sure," the portly man agreed, emphatically nodding. A bit of candied apple clung to his upper lip; he wiped it away with a freckled paw. "They got their rights, just like everybody else. Like you and me, mister . . . they got their lives, too."

Standing by the railing of the exhibit, the lean war veteran spoke up. "That don't apply to freaks. That's just people."

The portly man flushed. Waving his candied apple earnestly, he answered: "Mister, maybe they think *we're* freaks. Who says who's a freak?"

Disgusted, the veteran said: "I can tell a freak." He eyed Cussick and the portly man with distaste. "What are you," he demanded, "a freak-lover?"

The portly man sputtered and started over; but his wife seized his arm and dragged him away, into the crowd, to the next exhibits. Still protesting, he disappeared from sight. Cussick was left facing the war veteran.

"Damn fool," the veteran said. "It's contrary to common sense. You can see they're freaks. My God, that's why they're here!"

"He's right, though," Cussick pointed out. "The law gives anybody the right to live as he pleases. Relativism says—"

"Then the hell with Relativism. Did we fight a war, did we beat those Jews and atheists and Reds, so people could be any damn kind of freak they want? Believe any kind of egghead trash?"

"Nobody beat anybody," Cussick answered. "Nobody won the war."

A small knot of people had stopped to listen. The veteran noticed them; all at once his cold eyes faded and glazed over. He grunted, shot a last hostile look at Cussick, and melted off into the group. Dissappointed, the people moved on.

The next freak was part human, part animal. Somewhere along the line, inter-species mating had occurred; the event was certainly lost in the nightmarish shadows of the war. As he gazed up, Cussick tried to determine what the original progenitors had been; one, certainly, had been a horse. This freak, in all probability, was a fake, artificially grafted; but it was visually convincing. From the war had come intricate legends of man-animal progeny, exaggerated accounts of pure human stock that had degenerated, erotic tales of copulation between women and beasts.

There were many-headed babies, a common sport. He passed by the usual display of parasites living on sibling hosts. Feathered, scaled, tailed, winged humanoid freaks squeaked and fluttered on all sides: infinite oddities from ravaged genes. People with internal organs situated outside the dermal wall; eyeless, faceless, even headless freaks; freaks with enlarged and elongated and multi-jointed limbs; sad-looking creatures peeping out from within other creatures. A grotesque panorama of malformed organisms: dead-ends that would leave no spawn, monsters surviving by exhibiting their monstrous qualities.

In the main area, the entertainers were beginning their acts. Not mere freaks, but legitimate performers with skills and talents. Exhibiting not themselves, but rather their unusual abilities. Dancers, acrobats, jugglers, fire-eaters, wrestlers, fighters, animal-tamers, clowns, riders, divers, strong men, magicians, fortune-tellers, pretty girls . . . acts that had come down through thousands of years. Nothing new: only the freaks were new. The war brought new monsters, but not new abilities.

Or so he thought. But he hadn't seen Jones, yet. Nobody had; it was too early. The world went on rebuilding, reconstructioning: its time hadn't come.

To his left glared and winked the furious display of a girl exhibit. With some spontaneous interest, Cussick allowed himself to drift with the crowd.

Four girls lounged on the platform, bodies slack with ennui. One was clipping her nails with a pair of scissors; the others gazed vacantly at the crowd of men below. The four were naked, of course. In the weak sunlight their flesh glowed faintly luminous, oily, pale-pink, downy. The pitchman babbled metallically into his horn; his amplified voice thundered out in a garble of confused noise. Nobody paid any attention to the din; those who were interested stood peering up at the girls. Behind the girls was a closed sheet-tin building in which the show itself took place.

"Hey," one of the girls said.

Startled, Cussick realized she was speaking to him. "What?" he answered nervously.

"What time is it?" the girl asked.

Hurriedly, Cussick examined his wrist watch. "Eleven-thirty."

The girl wandered out of line, over to the edge of the platform. "Got a cigarette?" she asked.

Fumbling in his pocket, Cussick held up his pack.

"Thanks." Breasts bobbing, the girl crouched down and accepted a cigarette. After an uncertain pause, Cussick reached up his lighter and lit it for her. She smiled down at him, a small and very young woman, with brown hair and eyes, slim legs pale and slightly moist with perspiration. "You coming in to see the show?" she inquired.

He hadn't intended to. "No," he told her.

The girl's lips pulled together in a mocking pout. "No? Why not?" Nearby people watched with amusement. "Aren't you interested? Are you one of *those?*"

People around Cussick tittered and grinned. He began to feel embarrassment.

"You're cute," the girl said lazily. She settled down on her haunches, cigarette between her red lips, arms resting on her bare, out-jutting knees. "Don't you have fifty dollars? Can't you afford it?"

"No," Cussick answered, nettled. "Can't afford it."

"Aw." Teasing, pretending disappointment, the girl reached out her hand and rumpled his carefully-combed hair. "That's too bad. Maybe I'll take you on free. Would you like that? Want to be with me for nothing?" Winking, she stuck out the tip of a pink tongue at him. "I can show you a lot. You'd be surprised, the techniques I know."

"Pass the hat," a perspiring bald-headed man on Cussick's right chuckled. "Hey, let's get up a collection for this young fellow." A general stir of laughter drifted around, and a few five-dollar pieces were tossed forward.

"Don't you like me?" the girl was asking him, bending down and toward him, one hand resting on his neck. "Don't you think you could?" Taunting, coaxing, her voice murmured on: "I'll bet you could. And all these people think you could, too. They're going to watch. Don't you worry— I'll show you how." Suddenly she grabbed tight hold of his ear. "You just come on up here; mama'll show all of you people what she can do."

A roar of glee burst from the crowd, and Cussick was pushed forward and boosted up. The girl let go of his ear and reached with both hands to take hold of him; in that moment he twisted his way loose and dropped back down in the mass of people. After a short interval of shoving and running, he was standing beyond the crowd, panting for breath, trying to rearrange his coat . . . and his savoir faire.

Nobody was paying attention to him, so he began walking aimlessly along, hands in his pockets, as nonchalant as possible. People milled on all sides, most of them heading toward the main exhibits and the central area. Carefully, he evaded the moving flow; his best bet was the peripheral exhibits, open places where literature could be distributed and speeches made, tiny gatherings around a single orator. He wondered if the lean war veteran had been a fanatic; maybe he had identified Cussick as a cop.

The girl exhibit had been a sort of all-man's-land between freak and talent. Beyond the stage of girls stood the booth of the first fortuneteller, one of several.

"They're charlatans," the portly curly-haired man revealed to him; he was standing with his family by a dart-throwing booth, a handful of darts clutched, trying to win a twenty-pound Dutch ham. "Nobody can read the future; that's for suckers."

Cussick grinned. "So's a twenty-pound Dutch ham. It's probably made of wax."

"I'm going to win this ham," the man asserted good-naturedly. His wife said nothing, but his children displayed overt confidence in their father. "I'm going to take it home with me, tonight."

"Maybe I'll get my fortune told," Cussick said.

"Good luck, mister," the curly-headed man said charitably. He turned back to the dart target: a great eroded backdrop of the nine planets, pitted with endless near-misses. Its virgin center, an incredibly minute Earth, was untouched. The portly, curly-headed man drew back his arm and let fly; the dart, attracted by a deflecting concealed magnet, missed Earth and buried its steel tip in empty space a little past Ganymede.

At the first fortunetelling booth an old woman, dark-haired and fat, sat hunched over a squat table on which was arranged timeless apparatus: a transluscent globe. A few people were lined up on the stage, crowded in among the tawdry hangings waiting to pay their twenty dollars. A glaring neon sign announced:

YOUR FORTUNE READ   MADAME LULU CARIMA-ZELDA
KNOW THE FUTURE
BE PREPARED FOR ALL EVENTUALITIES

There was nothing here. The old woman mumbled through the traditional routine, satisfying the middle-aged women waiting in line. But next to Madame Lulu Carima-Zelda's booth was a second booth, shabby and ignored. A second fortuneteller, of sorts, sat here. But the bright glaring cheapness of Madame Carima-Zelda's booth had faded; the glittering nimbus died into gloomy darkness. Cussick was no longer walking through the shifting artificial fluorescent lights; he was standing in a gray twilight zone, between gaudy worlds.

On the barren platform sat a young man, not much older than himself, perhaps a little younger. His sign intrigued Cussick.

THE FUTURE OF MANKIND
(NO PERSONAL FORTUNES)

For an interval Cussick stood studying the young man. He was slouched in a sullen heap, smoking angrily and staring off into space. Nobody waited in line: the exhibit was ignored. His face was fringed with a stubbled beard; a strange face, swollen deep red, with bulging forehead, steel-rimmed glasses, puffy lips like a child's. Rapidly, he blinked, puffed on his cigarette, jerkily smoothed back his sleeves. His bare arms were pale and thin. He was an intent, sullen figure, seated alone on an empty expanse of platform.

No personal fortunes. An odd come-on for an exhibit;

nobody was interested in abstract fortunes, group fortunes. It sounded as if the teller wasn't much good; the sign implied vague generalities. But Cussick was interested. The man was licked before he started; and still he sat there. After all, fortunetelling was ninety-nine percent showmanship and the rest shrewd guesswork. In a carny he could learn the traditional ropes; why did he choose this offbeat approach? It was deliberate, obviously. Every line of the hunched, ugly body showed that the man intended to stick it out—*had* stuck it out, for God knew how long. The sign was shabby and peeling; maybe it had been years.

This was Jones. But at the time, of course, Cussick didn't know it.

Leaning toward the platform, Cussick cupped his hands and yelled: "Hey."

After a moment the youth's head turned. His eyes met Cussick's. Gray eyes, small and cold behind his thick glasses. He blinked and glared back, without speaking, without moving. On the table his fingers drummed relentlessly.

"Why?" Cussick demanded. "Why no personal fortunes?"

The youth didn't answer. Gradually his gaze faded; he turned his head and again glared down sightlessly at the table.

There was no doubt about it: this boy had no pitch, no line. Something was wrong; he was off-key. The other entertainers were hawking, yelling, turning themselves inside out (often literally) to attract attention, but this boy simply sat and glared. He made no move to get business; and he got none. Why, then, was he there?

Cussick hesitated. It didn't look like much of a place to snoop; actually, he was wasting the government's time. But his interest had been aroused. He sensed a mystery, and he didn't like mysteries. Optimistically, he believed things should be solved; he liked the universe to make sense. And this blatantly flaunted sense.

Climbing the steps, Cussick approached the youth. "All right," he said. "I'll bite."

The steps sagged under his feet; a rickety platform, unstable and unsafe. As he seated himself across from the youth, the chair groaned under him. Now that he was closer he could see that the youth's skin was mottled with deep splotches of color that might have been skin grafts. Had he been injured in the war? A faint odor of medicine hung about him, suggesting care of his frail body. Above the dome of his forehead his hair was tangled; his clothes clung in folds against his knobby frame. Now, he was peering up at Cussick, appraising him, warily studying him.

But not fearfully. There was an awkward crudeness about him, an uncertain twitch of his gaunt body. But his eyes were harsh and unyielding. He was gauche, but not afraid. It was no weak personality that faced Cussick; it was a blunt, determined young man. Cussick's own cheery bluster faded; he felt suddenly apprehensive. He had lost the initiative.

"Twenty dollars," Jones said.

Clumsily, Cussick fumbled in his pocket. "For what? What am I getting?"

After a moment Jones explained. "See that?" He indicated a wheel on the table. Pulling back a lever he released it; the hand on the wheel slowly turned, accompanied by a laborious metallic clicking. The face of the wheel was divided into four quarters. "You have one hundred and twenty seconds. Anything you want to ask. Then your time is up." He took the change and dropped it in his coat pocket.

"Ask?" Cussick said huskily. "About what?"

"The future." There was contempt in the youth's voice, undisguised, unconcealed. It was obvious; of course, the future. What else? Irritably, his thin hard fingers drummed. And the wheel ticked.

"But not personal?" Cussick pursued. "Not about myself?"

Lips twitching spasmodically, Jones shot back: "Of course not. You're a nonentity. You don't figure."

Cussick blinked. Embarrassed, feeling his ears begin to burn, he answered as evenly as possible: "Maybe you're wrong. Maybe I'm somebody." Hotly, he was thinking of his position; what would this rustic punk say if he knew he was facing a Fedgov secret-service man? It was on the tip of his tongue angrily to blurt it out, to give his role away in self-defense. That, of course, would finish him off with Security. But he was harried, and uncertain.

"You're down to ninety seconds," Jones notified him dispassionately. Then his gaunt, stony voice took on feeling. "For God's sake, *ask* something! Don't you want to know anything? Aren't you curious?"

Licking his lips, Cussick said: "Well, what's the future hold? What's going to happen?"

Disgusted, Jones shook his head. He sighed and stubbed out his cigarette. For a moment it seemed as if he wasn't going to answer; he concentrated on the smashed cigarette butt under the sole of his shoe. Then he dragged himself upright and carefully said: "Specific questions. Do you want me to think up one for you? All right, I will. Question. Who'll be the next Council chairman? Answer. The Nationalist candidate, a trivial individual named Ernest T. Saunders."

"But the Nationalists aren't a party! They're a cultist splinter-group!"

Ignoring him, Jones went on: "Question. What are the drifters? Answer. Beings from beyond the solar system, origin unknown, nature unknown."

Puzzled, Cussick hesitated. "Unknown up to what date?" he ventured. Plucking up his courage, he demanded: "How far can you see?"

Without particular inflection, Jones said: "I can see without error over a span of a year. After that, it fades. I can see major events, but specific details dim and I get nothing at all. As far as I can see ahead, the origin of the drifters is unknown." Glancing at Cussick, he added, "I mention them because they're going to be the big issue from now on."

"They already are," Cussick said, recalling the present sensational headlines in the cheap press: UNKNOWN FLIGHTS OF SHIPS DETECTED BY OUT-PLANET PATROLS. "You say they're beings? Not ships? I don't get it—you mean what we've sighted are the actual living creatures, not their artificially constructed—"

"Alive, yes," Jones interrupted impatiently, almost feverishly. "But Fedgov knows it already. Right now, at high level, they have detailed reports. The reports will be out in a few weeks; the bastards are withholding them from the public. A dead drifter was hauled in by a scout coming back from Uranus." Suddenly the wheel ceased clicking, and Jones dropped back in his chair, his flow of agitated words ceasing. "Your time is up," he announced. "If you want to know anything more, it'll be another twenty dollars."

Dazed, Cussick retreated away from him, down the steps and off the platform. "No thanks," he murmured. "That's plenty."

3

At four o'clock the police car picked him up and carried him back to Baltimore. Cussick was seething. Excitedly, he lit a cigarette, stubbed it out, and lit another. Maybe he had something; maybe not. The Baltimore secret-service buildings stood like a vast cube of concrete on the surface of the earth, a mile outside the city. Around the cube jutted metallic dots: coordinate block houses that were the mouths of elaborate subsurface tunnels. In the blue spring sky lazily flitted a few robot interception aerial mines. The police car slowed at the first check-station; guards carrying machine guns, with grenades bobbing at their belts, steel helmets glinting in the sun, strolled leisurely over.

An ordinary inspection. The car was passed; it made its way along a ramp and into the receiving area. At that point Cussick was dropped off; the car rolled into the garage, and he found himself standing alone before the ascent ramp, his mind still in turmoil. How was he supposed to evaluate what he had found?

Before he made his report to Security Director Pearson, he let himself off at one of the pedagogic levels. A moment later he was standing in the work-littered office of his Senior Political Instructor.

Max Kaminski was laboriously examining papers heaped over his desk. It was awhile before he noticed Cussick. "Home is the sailor," he remarked, continuing his work. "Home from the sea. And the hunter, too, for that matter. What did you bag out in the hills, this fine April afternoon?"

"I wanted to ask you something," Cussick said awkwardly. "Before I make my report." The tubby, round-faced man with his thick mustache and wrinkled brow had trained him; technically, Cussick was no longer under Kaminski's jurisdiction, but he still came for advice. "I know the law . . . but a lot depends on personal evaluation. There seems to be a statute violation, but I'm not certain which."

"Well," Kaminski said, putting down his fountain pen, removing his glasses, and folding his meaty hands, "as you know, violations fall into three main classifications. It's all based on Hoff's *Primer of Relativism;* I don't have to tell you that." He tapped the familiar blue-bound book at the edge of his desk. "Go read your copy again."

"I know it by heart," Cussick said impatiently, "but I'm still confused. The individual in question isn't asserting personal taste for statements of fact—he's making a statement about things unknowable."

"In particular?"

"About the future. He claims to know what's going to happen in the next year."

"Prediction?"

"Prophecy," Cussick corrected. "If I understand the distinction. And I claim prophecy is self-contradictory. Nobody can have absolute knowledge about the future. By definition, the future hasn't happened. And if knowledge existed, it would change the future—which would make the knowledge invalid."

"What was this, a fortuneteller at some carnival?"

Cussick colored. "Yes."

The older man's mustache quivered angrily. "And you're going to report it? You're going to recommend action against some entertainer trying to make a few dollars reading palms in a traveling circus? Over-zealous kids like you . . . *don't you understand how serious this is?* Don't you know what a conviction means? Loss of civil rights, confinement in a forced labor camp—" He shook his head. "So you can make a good impression on your superiors, some harmless fortuneteller is going to get the ax."

With controlled dignity, Cussick said: "But I think it's a violation of the law."

"Everybody violates the law. When I tell you olives taste terrible, I'm technically violating the law. When somebody says that dogs are man's best friend, it's illegal. It goes on all the time—we're not interested in that!"

Pearson had come into the office. "What's going on?" he demanded irritably, tall and stern in his brown police uniform.

"Our young friend here has brought back the quarry," Kaminski said sourly. "At this carnival he covered . . . he unearthed a fortuneteller."

Turning to Pearson, Cussick tried to explain. "Not a regular fortuneteller; there was one of those, too." Hearing his voice mutter out huskily, awkwardly, he rushed on: "I think this man's a mutant, a precog of some kind. He claims to know future history; he told me that somebody named Saunders is going to be the next Council chairman."

"Never heard of him," Pearson said, unimpressed.

"This man told me," Cussick went on, "that the drifters are going to turn out to be actual living creatures, not ships. And that it's known, now, at high levels."

A strange expression crossed Pearson's uncompromising features. At his desk, Kaminski abruptly stopped writing.

"Oh?" Pearson said faintly.

"He told me," Cussick continued, "that the drifters are going to be the biggest issue in the next year. The most important thing tangled with."

Neither Pearson nor Kaminski said anything. They didn't have to; Cussick could see it on their faces. He had made his point. He had covered all that was necessary.

Jones was about to become known.

4

As an immediate measure, Floyd Jones we taken into surveillance. That interim system continued for a period of seven months. In November of 1995, the bland, uncomplicated candidate of the extremist Nationalist Party came through and won the general Council election. Within twenty-four hours of the time Ernest T. Saunders was sworn into office, Jones had been quietly arrested.

In the half year, Cussick had lost most of his youthful plumpness. His face was firmer and older. He thought more, now, and talked less. And he had gained experience as a secret-service man.

In June of 1995, Cussick had been transferred to the Danish region. There he had met a pretty, buxom, and very independent Danish girl who worked in the art department of a Fedgov information center. Nina Longstren was the daughter of an influential architect; her people were wealthy, talented, and socially prominent. Even after they were officially married, Cussick still stood in awe of her.

His orders from police offices in Baltimore came while he and Nina were redoing their apartment. It took him a little while to find a way to bring the matter up; they were right in the middle of painting.

"Darling," he told her finally, "we're going to have to get the hell out of here."

For a moment Nina didn't answer. She was intently studying color charts, her elbows resting on the living room table, hands clasped under her chin. "What?" she murmured vaguely. The living room was a shambles of creativity; buckets of paint, rollers, sprayers lay everywhere. The furniture was covered with paint-splattered plastic sheeting. In the kitchen and bedrooms stood heaps of still-crated appliances, clothing, furniture, wrapped wedding presents. "I'm sorry . . . I wasn't listening."

Cussick walked over beside her and gently slid the color cards from under her elbows. "Orders from the big wheel. I have to fly back to Baltimore . . . they're assembling a case against this fellow Jones. I'm supposed to appear."

"Oh," Nina said faintly. "I see."

"It shouldn't take more than a couple of days. You can stay here, if you want." He didn't particularly want her to stay behind; they had only been married a week: technically, he was on his honeymoon. "They'll pay travel expenses for both of us—Pearson mentioned it."

"We really don't have much choice, do we?" Nina said forlornly. She got up from the table and began gathering together the various color cards. "I guess we should cover all the cans of paint."

Woebegone, she began pouring turpentine over a tin can of paint brushes. A smudge of sea-foam green was dabbed across her left cheek, probably as of when she had reached to push back her long blonde hair. Cussick took a rag, moistened it in the turpentine, and scrupulously removed the smudge.

"Thank you," Nina said sadly, when he had finished. "When do we have to leave? Right now?"

He examined his watch. "We better get into Baltimore by evening; they're holding him now. That means we ought to get the eight-thirty ship out of Copenhagen."

"I'll go bathe," Nina said obediently. "And change. You should, too." Critically, she rubbed his chin. "And shave."

He agreed. "Anything you want."

"Will you wear your light gray suit?"

"I have to wear brown. Remember, this is business. For the next twelve hours I'm back on the job."

"Does that mean we have to be solemn and serious?"

He laughed. "No, of course not. But this thing worries me."

Nina wrinkled her nose at him. "Worry, then. But don't expect me to. I've got other things to think about . . . you realize we won't get this place finished until next week?"

"We could get a couple of workmen in here to complete things."

"Oh, no," Nina said emphatically. She disappeared into the bathroom, turned on the hot water in the tub, and returned. Kicking off her shoes, she began undressing. "We're doing this ourselves. No broken-down tramps are getting in *this* apartment—this isn't a job; this is—" She searched for the words as she tugged her sweater up over her head. "This is our life together."

"Well," Cussick said dryly, "I was one of those broken-down tramps until I joined Security. But it's up to you. I enjoy painting; I don't care either way."

"You should care," Nina said critically. "Darn it, I'm going to spark some sort of artistic sensitivity in your bourgeois soul."

"Don't say I should care. That's a crime against Relativism. You can care all you want, but don't tell me I have to care, too."

Laughing, Nina skipped over and hugged him. "You great pompous thing. Taking it all so seriously—what am I going to do with you?"

"I don't know," Cussick admitted, frowning. "What are we going to do with all of us?"

"This thing really bothers you," Nina observed, gazing up into his face, her own blue eyes troubled and serious.

Cussick moved away from her and began assembling the heaps of newspapers scattered around the apartment. Nina watched, subdued and chastened, in her paint-streaked slacks and new nylon bra, feet bare, blonde hair tumbled loosely around her smooth shoulders. "Can you tell me anything about it?" she asked presently.

"Sure," Cussick said. Riffling the newspapers, he pulled one out, folded it, and handed it to her. "You can read about it while you're bathing."

The article was long and prominent.

MINISTER DRAWS CROWDS
FURTHER PROOF OF WORLD-WIDE RELIGIOUS REVIVAL
Citizens flock to hear minister tell of calamities to come. Infiltration by alien life-forms predicted in detail.

Below that was a picture of Jones, but no longer sitting on a platform in a side show. An ordained minister, now, wearing a shabby black frock coat, black shoes, more or less shaved, a Peripatetic preacher roaming about the countryside haranguing crowds of rustics. Nina glanced briefly at it, read a few words, glanced again at the picture, and then, without a word, turned and raced into the bathroom to shut off the water. She didn't return the newspaper; when next she appeared, ten minutes later, the newspaper had vanished.

"What'd you do with it?" Cussick asked curiously. He had fairly well straightened up the room and begun packing his suitcase.

"The newspaper?" Luminous and steaming from her bath, Nina began searching in the dresser for a fresh slip. "I'll read it later; right now we have to get packed."

"You don't really give a damn," Cussick said, with irritation.

"What about?"

"The work I'm doing. This whole system."

"Darling, it's none of my business." Tartly, she observed: "After all, it's supposed to be secret . . . I don't want to pry."

"Now listen," he said quietly. Going over to her he up-tilted her chin until she had to face him. "Sweetheart," he told her, "you knew what I was doing before you married me. This is no time to disapprove."

For a moment they faced each other defiantly. Then, with a swift dart of her hand, Nina swept up a perfume atomizer from the dresser and squirted him in the face. "Go shave and wash," she ordered him. "And for heaven's sake, put on a clean shirt—there's a whole drawer full of them. I want you to look nice, on the trip. I don't want to be ashamed of you."

Below the ship the blue, insipid expanse of the Atlantic lay spread out. Cussick restlessly scowled down at it, and then tried to interest himself in the TV screen glowing from the back of the seat before him. To his right, on the window side of him, dressed in an expensive hand-tailored worsted suit, Nina sat reading a copy of the *London Times* and daintily nibbling at a wafer-thin Swiss mint.

Moodily getting out his orders, Cussick began restudying the enclosed material. Jones had been arrested at four-thirty A.M. in the downstate section of Illinois, near a town called Pinckneyville. He had put up no resistance, as the police dragged him out of his wooden shack, described, technically, as his "church." Now he was being held in the main processing center at Baltimore. Presumably, a brief had already been drawn up by the Fedgov Attorney General's office; conviction was a matter of routine. There was the necessity of an appearance at the Public Court, and the actual sentencing . . .

"I wonder if he'll remember me," Cussick said aloud.

Nina lowered her *Times*. "What? I'm sorry, darling. I was reading the report of that scout ship that was grounded on Neptune for a month and three days. Lord, it must be awful out there. Those ice-cold planets, no air and no light, just dead rock."

"They're all useless," Cussick agreed testily. "It's a waste of the taxpayers' money to explore them." He folded up his orders and stuffed them away in his coat pocket.

"What's he like?" Nina asked. "Is he the one you told me about, the one who used to be a fortuneteller?"

"That's him."

"And they finally got around to arresting him?"

"It's not an easy thing."

"I thought it was all rigged; I thought you could get anybody."

"We can—but we don't want to. We only want people who seem to be dangerous. You think I'd arrest your brother's cousin because she goes around saying Beethoven quartets are the only music worth listening to?"

"You know," Nina said idly, "I don't remember a single thing I read in Hoff's book. We had it in school, of course. Required text in sociology." Blithely, she finished: "I just can't seem to get interested in Relativism . . . and now here I am married to a—" She glanced around. "I guess I shouldn't say. I still can't get used to this clandestine sneaking around."

"It's in a good cause," Cussick said.

Nina sighed. "I just wish you were in something else. In the shoelace business. Or even dirty postcards. Anything you could be proud of."

"I'm proud of this."

"Oh? Are you really?"

"I'm the town dog catcher," Cussick said soberly. "Nobody likes the dog catcher. Little kids pray a thunderbolt will strike the dog catcher. I'm the dentist. I'm the tax collector. I'm all the stern men who show up with folders of white paper, summoning people to face judgment. I didn't know that, seven months ago. I know it now."

"But you're still in the secret-service."

"Yes," Cussick said. "I still am. And I probably will be the rest of my life."

Nina hesitated. "Why?"

"Because Security is the lesser of two evils. I say evils. Of course, you and I know there's no such thing as evil. A glass of beer is evil at six in the morning. A dish of mush looks like hell around eight o'clock at night. To me, the spectacle of demagogues sending millions of people to their deaths, wrecking the world with holy wars and bloodshed, tearing down whole nations to put over some religious or political 'truth' is—" He shrugged. "Obscene. Filthy. Communism, Fascism, Zionism—they're the opinions of absolutist individuals forced on whole continents. And it has nothing to do with the sincerity of the leader. Or the followers. The fact that they believe it makes it even more obscene. The fact that they could kill each other and die voluntarily over meaningless verbalisms . . ." He broke off. "You see the reconstruction crews; you know we'll be lucky if we ever rebuild."

"But secret police . . . it seems so sort of ruthless and—well, and *cynical.*"

He nodded. "I suppose Relativism is cynical. It surely isn't idealistic. It's the result of being killed and injured and made poor and working hard for empty words. It's the outgrowth of generations of shouting slogans, marching with spades and guns, singing patriotic hymns, chanting, and saluting flags."

"But you put them into prison. These people who don't

agree with you—you won't *let* them disagree with
you . . . like this Minister Jones."

"Jones can disagree with us. Jones can believe anything he
wants; he can believe the Earth is flat, that God is an onion,
that babies are born in cellophane bags. He can have any
opinion he wants; but once he starts peddling it as Absolute
Truth—"

"Then you put him in prison," Nina said tightly.

"No," Cussick corrected. "Then we put out our hand; we
say simply: Put up or shut up. Prove what you're saying. If
you want to say the Jews are the root of all evil—*prove it*.
You can say it—if you can back it up. Otherwise, into the
work camp."

"It's—" She smiled a little. "It's a tough business."

"You bet it is."

"If you see me sipping cyanide through a straw," Nina
said, "you can't tell me not to. I'm free to poison myself."

"I can tell you it's cyanide in the bottle, not orange juice."

"But if I know?"

"Good God," Cussick said, "then it's your business. You
can bathe in it; you can freeze it and wear it. You're an adult."

"You—" Her lips quivered. "You don't care what happens
to me. You don't care if I take poison, or anything."

Cussick glanced at his wristwatch; the transport was already over the North American land mass. The trip was
virtually over. "I care. That's why I'm involved in this; I care
about you and the rest of suffering humanity." Broodingly,
he added: "Not that it matters. We flubbed Jones. This may
be the one time our bluff gets called."

"Why?"

"Right now we're saying to Jones: Put up; let's see the
proof. And I'm afraid the bastard's giving it to us."

In many ways Jones had changed. Standing silently in the
doorway, Cussick ignored the group of uniformed police

and studied the man sitting in the chair in the center of the room.

Outside the building a unit of police tanks rumbled along, followed by a regiment of weapons-troops. It was as if the presence of Jones had set off an uneasy chain of muscle-flexings. But the man himself paid no attention; he sat smoking, glaring down, his body taut. He sat very much as Cussick had seen him on the platform.

But he was older. The seven months had changed him, too. The ragged fringe of beard had grown; the man's face was ominous with coarse black hair, giving him an ascetic, almost spiritual quality. His eyes shone feverishly. Again and again he clasped his hands together, licked his dry lips, darted nervous, wary glances around the room. It occurred to Cussick that if he were really a precog, if he could really see a year ahead, he had anticipated this at the time Cussick had talked to him.

Abruptly Jones noticed him and glanced up. Their eyes met. Cussick began to perspire; he realized, chillingly, that as Jones had talked to him that day, as he had accepted his twenty dollars, he had seen this. Known that Cussick would turn in a report on him.

That meant, obviously, that Jones was here voluntarily.

From a side door Director Pearson appeared, a sheaf of papers clutched in his hand. He stalked over to Cussick, boots and helmet shining, impressive in his full uniform. "We're all bobbled up," he said, without preamble. "We sat on our behinds waiting to find out if the rest of his gabble worked out. It did. It did. So now we're stuck."

"I could have told you that." Cussick reflected. "In seven months of surveillance, didn't you get a whole boatful of prophecies?"

"We did. But the brief was drawn up on this; the Saunders one is the basis of our case. You heard the official release of data on the drifters, of course."

"It filtered in while I was on my honeymoon. I didn't particularly care, not at the time."

Lighting his pipe, Pearson said: "We ought to buy up this fellow. But he says he's not for sale."

"This really is it, isn't it? He's not a fake."

"No, he's not a fake. And the whole damn system is based on the theory that he *has* to be a fake. Hoff never took this into account; this spellbinder is telling the truth." Taking hold of Cussick's arm he led him through the circle of police. "Come on over and say hello. Maybe he'll remember you."

Jones watched rigidly, as the two men made their way toward him. He recognized Cussick; there was no ambiguity in his expression.

"Hello," Cussick said. Jones got slowly to his feet and they faced each other. Presently Jones put out his hand, and they shook. "How have you been?"

"Fine," Jones replied noncommittally.

"You knew about me, that day. You knew I was in Secpol."

"No," Jones disagreed. "As a matter of fact I didn't."

"But you knew you'd be here," Cussick said, surprised. "You must have seen this room, this meeting."

"I didn't recognize you. You looked different, then. You don't realize how much you've changed in the last seven months. All I knew was that somewhere along the line a contact was made with me." He spoke dispassionately, but tensely. A muscle in his cheek twitched. "You've lost weight . . . but sitting around behind a desk hasn't improved your posture."

"What are you doing these days?" Cussick asked. "You're not with the carnival?"

"I'm a minister of the Honorable Church of God," Jones said, with a wry spasm.

"You look pretty seedy for a minister."

Jones shrugged. "It doesn't pay very well. Right now, not too many people are interested." He added, "But they will be."

"You know, of course," Pearson broke in, "that this whole interview is being taped. Everything you say is going to be played back at the trial."

"What trial?" Jones commented brutally. "Three days from now you're going to release me." Thin face twitching, his voice cold and bleak, he continued thoughtfully, "From now on you're going to be telling a certain parable. I'll tell it, now; pay attention. An Irishman hears that the banks are failing. He runs into the bank where he keeps his money and demands every cent of it. 'Yes sir,' the teller says politely. 'Do you want it in cash or in the form of a check?' The Irishman replies: 'Well, if you have it, I don't want it. But if you haven't got it, I must have it immediately.' "

There was an uncomfortable silence. Pearson looked puzzled; he glanced at Cussick. "Am I going to tell that?" he asked doubtfully. "What's it mean?"

"It means," Cussick said, "that nobody's fooling anybody."

Jones smiled in appreciation.

"Am I to infer," Pearson said, his face turning dark and ugly, "that you think we can't do anything to you?"

"I don't *think*," Jones answered smugly. "I don't have to. That's the point. Do you want my prophecies in cash or in the form of a check? Take your choice."

Thoroughly bewildered, Pearson moved away. "I can't understand him," he muttered. "He's a crackpot; he's out of his mind."

"No," Senior Political Instructor Kaminski said. He had been standing nearby, intently listening. "You're an odd person, Jones," he said to the bony-shanked man standing nervously by the chair. "What I can't understand is this. With your ability, why were you fooling around in that carnival? Why were you wasting your time?"

Jones' answer surprised them all. Its candor, its naked honesty, was a shock. "Because I'm scared," he said. "I don't know what to do. And the awful part is—" He swallowed noisily. "I don't have any choice."

5

In Kaminski's office the four of them sat around the desk, smoking, and dully hearing the distant mutter of police guns on their way to the staging area.

"To me," Jones said hoarsely, *"this is the past.* Right now, with you three, here in this building, this is a year ago. It's not so much like I can see the future; it's more that I've got one foot stuck in the past. I can't shake it loose. I'm retarded; I'm reliving one year of my life forever." He shuddered. "Over and over again. Everything I do, everything I say, hear, experience, I have to grind over twice." He raised his voice, sharp and anguished, without hope. "I'm living the same life two times!"

"In other words," Cussick said slowly, "for you, the future is static. Knowing about it doesn't make it possible for you to change it."

Jones laughed icily. "Change it? It's totally fixed. It's more fixed, more permanent, than this wall." Furiously, he slammed his open palm against the wall behind him. "You think I've some kind of emancipation. Don't kid yourself . . . the less you know about the future the better off you are. You've got a nice illusion; you think you have free will."

"But not you."

"No," Jones agreed bitterly. "I'm trudging along the steps I trudged a year ago. I can't alter a single one of them. This conversation—I know it by heart. Nothing new can come into it; nothing can be left out."

After a moment Pearson spoke up. "When I was a kid," he reflected, "I used to go to movies twice. The second time, it gave me an advantage over the rest of the audience . . . I liked it. I could holler out the dialogue a split second before the actors. It gave me a sense of power."

"Sure," Jones agreed. "When I was a kid I liked it, too. But I'm not a kid anymore. I want to live like everybody else—an ordinary life. I didn't ask for this; it wasn't my idea."

"It's a valuable talent," Kaminski said shrewdly. "As Pearson says, a man who can shout out the dialogue a split second ahead of time has real power. He's a whole notch above the rest of the crowd."

"The thing I remember," Pearson said, "is the contempt I felt for all the rapt faces. The fools—staring, simpering, giggling, being afraid, believing in it, wondering how it would come out. And I knew. It made me disgusted. That's partly why I shouted it out."

Jones didn't comment. Brooding, he sat hunched over in his chair, eyes fixed on the floor.

"How would you like a job?" Kaminski inquired dryly. "Senior Political Instructor to the Senior Political Instructor."

"No thanks."

"You could be a lot of help," Pearson pointed out. "You could aid reconstruction. You could help us unify ourselves and our resources. You could make an important difference."

Jones shot him an exasperated glare. "There's only one

issue of importance. This reconstruction—" He waved his thin, bony hand impatiently. "You're wasting your time . . . it's the drifters that matter."

"Why?" Cussick demanded.

"Because there's a whole universe! You spend your time rebuilding this planet—my God, we could have a million planets. New planets, untouched planets. Systems of them. Endless resources . . . and you sit around trying to remelt old scrap. Pack rats, misers, boarding and fingering your miserable pile." Disgusted, he turned away. "We're overpopulated. We're undernourished. One more habitable world would solve all that."

"Like Mars?" Cussick inquired softly. "Like Venus? Dead, empty, hostile worlds."

"I don't mean those."

"What do you mean, then? We've got scouts crawling all around the system. Show us one place we can live."

"Not here." Angrily, Jones dismissed the solar system. "I mean out there. Centaurus. Or Sirius. Any of them."

"Are they necessarily any better?"

"Intersystem colonization is possible," Jones answered. "Why do you think the drifters are here? It's obvious— they're settling. They're doing what we should be doing: they're out searching for habitable planets. They may have come millions of light years."

"Your answer isn't good enough," Kaminski pronounced.

"It's good enough for me," Jones said.

"I know." Kaminski nodded, troubled. "That's what worries me."

Curiously, Pearson asked: "Do you know anything more about the drifters? Who shows up in the next year?"

Across Jones' face settled a stark, impassioned glaze. "That's why I'm a minister," he said harshly.

The three secret-servicemen waited, but there was nothing more. *Drifters* was a key word with Jones; visibly, the word triggered off something deep and basic inside him. Something that made his gaunt face writhe. A core of blazing fervor had floated to the surface.

"You don't particularly like them," Cussick observed.

"Like them?" Jones looked ready to explode. "Drifters? Alien life-forms coming here, settling on our planets?" His voice rose to a shrill, hysterical screech. "Can't you see what's happening? How long do you think they'll leave us alone? Eight dead worlds—nothing but rock. And Earth: *the only useful one.* Don't you see? They're preparing to attack us; they're using Mars and Venus as bases. It's Earth they're after; who'd want those empty wastes?"

"Maybe they do," Pearson suggested uneasily. "As you said, they're alien life-forms. Maybe to them Earth is nothing. Maybe they need totally different living-conditions."

Eying Jones intently, Kaminski said: "Every life-form has its own typical needs . . . what's a ruined waste to us is a fertile valley to something else. Isn't that so?"

"Earth is the only fertile planet," Jones repeated, with absolute conviction. "They want Earth. That's what they're here for."

Silence.

So that was it. There it stood, the terrifying spectre they all dreaded. This was what they existed to destroy; this was what they had been set up to catch—before it was too big to catch. It stood before them; sat, rather. Jones had again seated himself; now he sat smoking jerkily, thin face distorted, a dark vein in his forehead pulsing. Behind his glasses his furiously-bright eyes had filmed over, cloudy with passion. Tangled hair, ragged black beard, a rumpled man with elongated arms, skinny legs . . . a man with infinite power. A man with infinite hatred.

"You really hate them," Cussick said wonderingly.

Mutely, Jones nodded.

"But you don't know anything about them, do you?"

"They're there," Jones said brittlely. "They're all around us. Encircling us. Closing in. Can't you see their plans? Coming across space, century after century . . . working out their schemes, landing first on Pluto, on Mercury, coming closer all the time. Nearer to the prize: setting up bases for attack."

"Attack," Kaminski repeated softly, cunningly. "You know this? You have proof? Or is this just a wild idea?"

"Six months from this date," Jones stated, his voice pinched and metallic, "the first drifter will land on Earth."

"Our scouts have landed on all the planets," Kaminski pointed out, but his silky assurance was gone. "Does that mean we're invading them?"

"We're there," Jones said, "because those planets are ours. We're looking them over." Raising his eyes, he finished: "And that's what the drifters are doing. They're looking over Earth. Right now, they're looking us over. Can't you feel their eyes on us? Filthy, loathsome, alien, insect eyes . . ."

Horrified, Cussick said: "He's pathological."

"Can you *see* this?" Kaminski pursued.

"I know it."

"But you *see* it? You see an invasion? Destruction? Drifters taking over Earth?"

"Within a year," Jones stated, "there'll be drifters landing everywhere. Every day of the week. Ten here, twenty there. Hordes of them. All identical. Mindless hordes of filthy alien beings."

With an effort, Pearson said: "Sitting next to us in busses, I take it. Wanting to marry our daughters—right?"

Jones must have anticipated the remark; a second before Pearson spoke, the man's face went chalk-white, and he gripped convulsively at the arms of his chair. Fighting with himself, struggling to keep control, he answered between his teeth: "People aren't going to stand for it, friend. I can see that. There's going to be burnings. Those drifters are dry, friend. They burn well. There's going to be lots of cleaning up to do."

Kaminski swore softly, furiously. "Let me out of here," he began saying, to nobody in particular. "I can't stand it."

"Take it easy," Pearson said sharply.

"No, I can't stand it." Futilely, Kaminski paced around in a circle. "There's nothing we can do! We can't touch him— he really sees these things. He's safe from us—*and he knows it.*"

It was early night. Cussick and Pearson stood together in the dark corridor of the top floor of the police offices. A few paces away a dispatch carrier waited, his face bland beneath his steel helmet.

"Well," Pearson began. He shivered. "This hall is cold. Why don't you and your wife come over to my place for dinner? We can talk, sit around, discuss things."

Cussick said: "Thanks, I'd like to. You haven't met Nina."

"I understand you were on leave. Honeymoon?"

"Sort of. We've got a nice little place in Copenhagen . . . we had started painting it."

"How'd you find a place?"

"Nina's family put their shoulder to the wheel."

"Your wife's not in Security, is she?"

"No. Art and idealism."

"What's she think about you being a cop?"

"She doesn't like it. She wonders if it's necessary. The new tyranny." Ironically, Cussick added: "After all, absolutists are dying out. In a few more years—"

"Do you think Hitler was a precog?" Pearson asked suddenly.

"Yes, I do. Not as developed as Jones, of course. Dreams, hunches, intuitions. The future was fixed for him, too. And he took long chances. I think Jones will begin taking long chances, too. Now that he's beginning to understand what he's here on Earth for."

In Pearson's hand was a flat document. Idly, he tapped it against his fingers. "You know what crazy notion entered my mind? I was going down there where they're holding him, down in that room. I was going to pry open his jaws and drop an A-pellet down his throat. Blow his carcass to fragments. But then I got to thinking."

"He can't be killed," Cussick said.

"He *can* be killed. But he can't be taken by surprise. To kill Jones would mean bottling him up from all sides. He's got a one-year jump on us. He'll die; he's mortal. Hitler died, finally. But Hitler slithered away from a lot of bullets and poisons and bombs in his time. It'll take a closing ring to do it . . . a room with no doors. And you can tell by the look on his face that there's still a door."

He called the dispatch carrier over.

"Deliver this personally. You know where—downramp at 45A. Where they've got that skinny dried-up hick."

The carrier saluted, accepted the document, and trotted briskly off.

"You think he believes all that?" Pearson wondered. "About the drifters?"

"We'll never know. He's got something big, there. Naturally, they're going to land; they propel themselves randomly, don't they?"

"As a matter of fact," Pearson said, "one has landed already."

"Alive?"

"Dead. Research is working on it. Apparently the secret will stay kept—until the next one."

"Can they tell anything about it?"

"Quite a bit. It's a gigantic, single-celled organism using empty space as a culture medium. It drifts, using some kind of vague propulsion mechanism. It's absolutely harmless. It's an amoeba. It's twenty feet wide. It's got some kind of tough rind to keep out the cold. This is no sinister invasion; these poor goddamn things just wander mindlessly around."

"What do they eat?"

"They don't. They just go on until they die. There's no feeding mechanism, no digestive process, no excretion, no reproductive apparatus. They're incomplete."

"Odd."

"Apparently, we've run into a swarm of them. Sure, they've started falling. They'll hit here and there, burst apart, smack into cars, flatten themselves out in fields. Foul up lakes and streams. They'll be a pest. They'll stink and flop. More likely, just lie quietly dying. Baking away in the sun . . . heat killed this one: baked it to a crisp. And meanwhile, people will have something to think about."

"Especially when Jones gets started."

"If it wasn't Jones, it'd be somebody else. But Jones has that talent, that advantage. He can call the shots."

"That document was his release papers, wasn't it?"

"That's right," Pearson said. "He's free. Until we can think up a new law, he's a free man. To do as he pleases."

6

In the tiny, white-gleaming, ascetic police cell, Jones stood swabbing the inside of his mouth with Dr. Sherrif's Special Throat Tonic. The tonic was bitter and unpleasant. He rolled it from cheek to cheek, held it in the upper portion of his trachea for a moment, and then spat it into the porcelain washbowl.

Without comment, the two uniformed policemen, one at each end of the chamber, watched. Jones paid no attention to them; peering into the mirror over the bowl, he scrupulously combed his hair. Then he rubbed the side of his thumb over his teeth. He wanted to be in shape; in an hour he was going to be involved in important matters.

For a moment he tried to remember what came immediately ahead. The release notice was due, or so he thought. It was so long ago; one whole year had passed and details had blurred. Vaguely, he had memory of a cop entering with something, a paper of some kind. That was it: that was the release. And after that came a speech.

The speech was still clear in his mind; he hadn't forgotten it. Annoyance came, as he thought about it. Giving the same words again, repeating the same gestures. The old mechan-

ical actions . . . stale events, dry and dusty, sagging under
the smothering blanket of dull age.

And meanwhile, the living wave flashed on.

He was a man with his eyes in the present and his body in
the past. Even now, as he stood examining his grubby clothes,
smoothing his hair, rubbing his gums, even as he stood here
in the antiseptic police cell, his senses were glued tight on
another scene, a world that still danced with vitality, a world
that hadn't become stale. Much had happened in the next
year. And as he scraped peevishly at his bearded chin, plucking at an old rash, the wave uncovered new moments, new
excitements and events.

The wave of the future was washing up incredible shells
for him to examine.

Impatiently, he strode to the door of the chamber and
peered out. That was what he hated; that was the loathsome
thing. The molasses of time: it couldn't be hurried. On it
dragged, with weary, elephantine steps. Nothing could urge
it faster: it was monstrous and deaf. Already, he had exhausted the next year; he was totally tired of it. But it was
going to take place anyhow. Whether he liked it or not—and
he didn't—he was going to have to relive each inch of it, re-
experience in body what he had long ago known in mind.

Such had been happening all his life. The misphasing had
always existed. Until he was nine years old, he had imagined
that every human being endured duplication of all waking
instants. At nine, he had lived out eighteen years. He was
exhausted, disgusted, and fatalistic. At nine and a half years,
he discovered that he was the only individual so burdened.
From then on, his resignation rapidly became raging
impatience.

He was born in Colorado, August 11, 1977. The war was
still in progress, but it had bypassed the American Middle
West. The war had not bypassed Greeley, Colorado; it had
never come there. No war could reach into every town, to

every living human being. The farm which his family maintained continued almost as usual; a self-sufficient economic unit, it carried on with its stagnant routine, ignorant of and indifferent to the crisis of mankind.

First memories were bizarre. Later, he had attempted to untangle them. The languid foetus had entertained impressions of a notyet world; as he crouched curled up in his mother's bloated womb, a phantasmagoria, incomprehensible and vivid, had swirled around him. Simultaneously, he had lain in the bright sunshine of a Colorado autumn and dreamed quietly in the black moist sack, the dripping all-provider. He had known birth terror before he was conceived; by the time the embryo was a month old, the trauma was long in the past. The actual event of birth was of no significance to him; as he was swung suspended from the doctor's fist, he had already been in the world one full year.

They wondered why the new baby failed to cry. And why his learning process was so rapid.

Once, he had conjectured this way: what was the real moment of his origin? At what point in time had he really come into being? Floating in the womb, he had clearly been alive, sentient. To what had the first memories come? One year before birth, he had not been a unit, not even a zygote; the elements that comprised him had not come together. And by the time the fertilized egg had begun to divide, the wall had carried well beyond the moment of birth: three months into the hot, dusty, bright Colorado fall.

It was a mystery. He finally stopped thinking about it.

In his early years of childhood he had accepted his dual existence, learned to integrate the two continua. The process had not been easy. For months he had laboriously crept head-on into doors, furniture, walls. He had reached for a spoon of Pablum one year hence; he had fretfully declined a nipple long ago forgotten. Confusion had virtually starved him to death; he had been force-fed, and forcibly prevented from wandering out of existence. Naturally, it was assumed that he was feeble-minded. A baby that groped for invisible objects, that tried to put its hands through the side of its crib . . .

But at four months he was saying complete words.

Scenes from his childhood, reinforced by double occurrence, had never left his mind. One of them leaped up now, as he stood in the white, sanitary police cell, impatiently waiting for his release papers. When he was nine and a half, the first hydrogen bomb had arrived. Not the first hydrogen bomb dropped in the war; dozens had fallen throughout the world. This was the first to penetrate the intricate screens guarding the heartland of America, the region from the Rocky Mountains to the Mississippi. The bomb had detonated a hundred miles from Greeley. Radioactive ash and particles had drifted mercilessly across the countryside for weeks after, sickening the cattle and withering the crops. From the death zone, trucks and cars laboriously carted off the sick and mutilated. Repair crews made their way forward to inspect the vast damage. To seal off the titanic sore until it had given up its load of toxins . . .

Along the narrow dirt road past the Jones' farm passed a seemingly endless convoy of emergency vehicles, on their way to hospitals and wards erected outside of Denver. Going the other way moved a flow of supplies for the survivors remaining in the blighted area. All this, he had watched with fascination. From morning to night there was no let-up in the streams of cars, trucks, ambulances, people on foot, people on bicycles, dogs, cattle, sheep, chickens, a motley pack of shapes and colors and sounds; distant groans that reached the boy's ear and sent him excitedly rushing into the house.

"What is it?" he screamed, dancing wildly around his mother.

His mother, Mrs. Edna Jones, paused by the laundry tubs, her gray face wrinkled with fatigue and annoyance. She tossed back her grime-soaked hair and turned crossly to the boy. "What are you babbling about?" she demanded.

"The cars!" he shouted, dancing to the window and pointing out. "See them? Who are they? What is it?"

Outside the window there was nothing. Nothing for her, at least; she couldn't see what the boy saw.

Scampering outside, he stood gazing at the line moving along the horizon, outlined by the setting sun. On and on they moved . . . where were they going? What had happened to them? He ran to the edge of the farm, as far as it was permitted. Wire barred his way, a tangle of rusty barbs. Almost, he could make out individual faces; almost, he could penetrate the sight of individual pain. If only he could get closer . . .

This was the moment of his awakening. Because he alone saw the procession of doom. To all others, even to the doomed themselves, it was not there. He recognized a face: old Mrs. Lizzner, from Denver. She was there. Faces he knew, people he had seen in church. They were not strangers; they were neighbors, local people. They were the world, *his* world, the shrunken, dried-up Middle Western world.

The next day Mrs. Lizzner drove up to the farm in her dusty Oldsmobile, to spend an afternoon with his mother.

"Did you see?" he shouted at her. "Did you see it?"

She hadn't seen it. And she had been a part of it. So there was no doubt; there was no point in pursuing the issue further.

Real understanding came in his tenth year. Now the bomb had come; Mrs. Lizzner was dead, and the area had in reality been laid waste. Such a unique cataclysm, never repeated, never seen before or since, was unmistakable. What he alone had seen had now swallowed up everyone. The relationship of the wave to what his fellow humans experienced was obvious. Of course, he told no one. As comprehension came, his attempts to communicate ceased.

He could not go back. Knowing that he was different, he could not return to the aimless activity of the farm. The monotony of farm chores was doubled for him; it was too much of a burden. At fifteen, gaunt and bony and brooding, he had collected his funds (perhaps two hundred dollars, all Westbloc inflation currency) and departed.

He found the Denver area painfully recovering from the blast. That was expected, as was everything else. One year before, at fourteen, he had previewed his journey. Once again, but this time at first hand, he examined the gaping crater the bomb had left, conjectured on the thousands of people who had been turned to ash in the wink of an eye. He boarded a bus and left Colorado. Three days later he was in the ruins of Pittsburgh.

Here, basic industrial activities continued. Underground, the forges still bellowed. But Jones wasn't interested; on foot he continued his journey, past the smoldering miles of metal that had once been the greatest concentrate of factories in the universe. Military law prevailed; as he had previewed, patrols encountered him and swept him up in the general net.

At the age of fifteen years and three months he was examined by competent authorities, questioned, fingerprinted, and disposed of. The labor battalion he joined caused him no surprise; but the anguish remained. Grimly, wrathfully, he carried handfuls of rock for months on end, trying, with a company of others, to clear the ruins by the most primitive of means. By the end of the year, machinery had been brought in, and the hand-work disbanded. He was older, stronger, and considerably wiser. Just about the time he was given a gun and moved toward the crumbling lines, the war ended.

He had foreseen that. Slipping away from his unit, he traded in his rifle for a good meal and destroyed his military uniform. A day later he was tramping the highway as he had begun: on foot, in jeans and tattered sweatshirt, a pack on his back, wandering through the tumble of debris that had survived the war, the chaotic desolation that was the new world.

For almost seventeen years his dual existence had been purposeless. It had been a burden, a great dead weight. Even the idea of utilizing it was lacking. He saw it as a cross, nothing more. Life was painful; his was twice painful. What good was it to know that the misery of the next year was unavoidable? If Mrs. Lizzner had seen her dying remains carted along the road, would she have been better off?

Somebody had to teach him to use his talent; somebody had to show him how to exploit it.

That person was a fat, perspiring salesman in a pink-stripe shirt and lemon-yellow dacron trousers, driving a battered Buick. The back seat of the car was crowded with slender brown boxes, great piles and heaps of them. Jones, hunched with fatigue, was creeping along the dusty shoulder of the road, when the Buick snarled to a steaming halt. Having boarded the car a year ago, he scarcely looked up. Yanking his pack around, he turned and stolidly climbed in beside the driver.

"You don't seem very grateful," Hyndshaw muttered resentfully, as he started up the car. "You want to get back out, sonny?"

Jones lay back against the tattered upholstery and rested. For him, the sequence ahead was visible; Hyndshaw was not going to throw him out. Hyndshaw was going to talk: he liked to talk. And in that talk, something of great value was coming for the boy.

"Where you going?" Hyndshaw demanded curiously. Between his lips jutted the wet stump of a cigar. His fingers daintily plucked at the power-driven wheel. His eyes, deep-set in fat, were wise with cunning of the world. Beer stains discolored the bib of his shirt. He was a sloppy, easy-going, vice-saturated creature, smelling of sweat and years of wandering travel. And he was a great, dreaming swindler.

"Nowhere," Jones said, answering his question with his usual sullen indifference. He had been tired of the question for twelve months.

"Sure, you're going somewhere," Hyndshaw opined.

And then the event happened. Words, actions, taking place at the perimeter of the moving wave, had become eternally fixed. One year ago, the exhausted boy had uttered a brusque, thoughtless remark. He had had the interval to reap the provocative harvest from that remark.

"Don't tell me where I'm going," he shot back. "I can see; I can see where you're going, too."

"Where'm I going?" Hyndshaw retorted testily; he was on his way to a nearby house of ill repute, and the area was still under military jurisdiction.

Jones told him.

"How do you know?" Hyndshaw demanded hoarsely, breaking into Jones' detailed account of the man's forthcoming activity. "You goddamn foul-mouthed kid—" White and frightened, he shouted: "What are you, a goddamn mind reader?"

"No," Jones answered. "But I'm going along. I'll be with you."

That sobered Hyndshaw even more. For a time he didn't talk; unnerved, he clenched the wheel and glared ahead at the pitted, dilapidated road. Here and there, on each side, were the abandoned shells of houses. This region, around St. Louis, had been forcibly evacuated after a successful shower of Soviet bacterial pellets. The inhabitants were still in forced labor camps, rebuilding more vitally needed areas; industrial and agricultural production came first.

Hyndshaw was frightened, but at the same time his natural

greed and interest grew. He was a born opportunist. God knew what he had stumbled on. He decided to proceed cautiously.

"You know what I've got back there?" he said, indicating the piles of slender cartons. "Give you three guesses."

The concept *guess* was alien to Jones. "Magnetic belts," he answered. "Fifty dollars retail, forty dollars in lots of ten or more. Guaranteed to ward off toxic radioactivity and bacterial poisons or your money back."

Licking his lips nervously, Hyndshaw asked: "Did I already talk to you? Maybe up around the Chicago area?"

"You're going to try to sell me one. When we stop for water."

Hyndshaw hadn't intended to stop for water; he was late as it was. "Water?" he muttered. "Why water? Who's thirsty?"

"The radiator's leaking."

"How do you know?"

"In fifteen minutes—" Jones reflected; he had forgotten the exact interval. "In around half an hour your temperature gauge is going to flash, and you're going to have to stop. You'll find water at an abandoned well."

"You know all that?"

"Of course I know all that." Irritably, Jones tore a loose strip of cloth from the upholstery. "Would I be saying it if I didn't?"

Hyndshaw said nothing. He sat driving silently until, after twenty or so minutes, the temperature gauge flashed, and he brought the Buick quickly to the side of the road.

The only sound was the unhappy wheezing of the empty radiator. A few wisps of oil smoke curled upward from the vents of the hood.

"Well," Hyndshaw muttered shakily, fumbling for the door handle. "I guess we better start looking. Which way you say that well is?"

Because he didn't have to guess, Jones found the well instantly. It was half-buried under a heap of stone, brick, and slats that had been a barn. Together, the two of them lowered a rusty bucket. Ten minutes later Hyndshaw was opening bottles of warm beer and showing off one of his magnetic belts.

As he babbled his pitch, his mind raced furiously. Here was something. He had heard of mutants, even seen them. Hideous freaks, most of them; deformed monstrosities systematically destroyed by the authorities. But this was something else; this was no oddity. Anybody who could eliminate surprises, who could cut through guesswork . . .

That was why Hyndshaw made a good salesman. He was a good guesser. But he could guess wrong; he could misevaluate a situation. Not so with the youth beside him. They both knew it. Hyndshaw was fascinated and impressed. Jones was contemptuous.

"How much money have you got?" Hyndshaw demanded suddenly, interrupting his own pitch. Cunningly, he conjectured: "You haven't got fifty bucks to your name. You couldn't afford one of these belts."

"I've got fifty bucks," Jones said, "but not for a cheap piece of fakery."

Hyndshaw spluttered; in years of preying on ignorant rural populations, made even more fearful and superstitious by the war, he had come to believe his own lies. "What do you mean?" he began, and then shut up, as Jones told him.

"I see," Hyndshaw said, when the short, bitter tirade was done. "You're quite a kid . . . you're not afraid to say what you think."

"Why should I be?"

Tightly, Hyndshaw said: "Maybe somebody might kick your smart teeth down your throat, one of these days. Your wise-guy talk might not sit right with somebody . . . they might resent a punk kid."

"Not you," Jones told him. "You're not going to lay a hand on me.

"What, then?"

"You're going to propose we go into business together. Your stock of belts and experience—my ability. Fifty-fifty."

"Belts? You're coming in with me on the belt business?"

"No," Jones answered. "That's your idea. I'm not interested in belts. We're going into bone-throwing."

Hyndshaw was baffled. "What's that?"

"Gambling. Dice. Craps."

"I don't know anything about gambling." Hyndshaw was deeply suspicious. "You're sure this is on the level? You're sure this isn't a goddamn come-on?"

Jones didn't bother to answer; he continued what he had been saying. "We'll operate a concession at this cat house for maybe a month or so. You'll get most of the take; I'm not interested.Then we'll split up. You'll try to stop me and I'll turn the whole place in to the military police. The girls will be sent to labor camps, you'll go to prison."

Horrified, Hyndshaw gasped: "God, I don't want anything to do with you." He grabbed up a beer bottle and smashed it against a nearby rock; the jagged teeth of glass oozed damp foam as he clutched the weapon convulsively. Repelled by the boy, he was nearing a point of hysteria. "You're crazy!" he shouted, half-lifting the bottle in an innate gesture of defense.

"Crazy?" Jones was puzzled. "Why?"

Jerkily, Hyndshaw gestured. Cold sweat leaked off his face, into his open collar. "You're telling me this? You sit there telling me what you're going to do to me?"

"It's the truth."

Tossing the bottle away, Hyndshaw savagely yanked the boy to his feet. "Don't you know anything but the truth?" he snarled, in despair.

No, he didn't. How could he? For Jones there was no

guessing, no error, and no false knowledge. He knew; he had absolute certainty. "Take it or leave it," he said, shrugging indifferently. He had already lost interest in the fat salesman's fate; after all, it had happened a long time ago. "Do whatever you want."

Gripping the boy futilely, Hyndshaw bellowed: "You know I'm stuck. You know I don't have a choice. You can see it!"

"Nobody has a choice," Jones said, suddenly stern and thoughtful. "Not me or you—nobody. We're all chained up like cattle. Like slaves."

Slowly, wretchedly, Hyndshaw let go of him. "Why?" he protested, raising his fat, empty hands.

"I don't know. That's something I can't tell you—yet." Jones calmly finished his beer and then tossed the bottle into the dry weeds at the edge of the road. In the last year the weeds had grown six feet high. "Let's go—I'm interested in getting into this cat house. It'll be the first time for me."

Into the hygenic police cell stepped the dispatch carrier. He saluted the guards and handed over his papers.

"All right," one of the guards said, nodding to Jones. "Come along."

The wait was over; he was on his way. Exultant, Jones followed after the clanking, uniformed figure. The guard led him down a long yellow-lit corridor, to a series of magnetically-sealed locks. The locks rolled back, and beyond lay an ascending ramp lost in cold night shadow. A dark wind whipped along the ramp, plucking at Jones' sleeves. Overhead chill stars shone here and there, set in a totally opaque sky.

He was outside the police building.

At the terminus of the ramp stretched a concrete driveway. A few yards off to one side a heavy car stood gleaming, moist and metallic. The guard led him to it, held the door open, and then slid in beside him. The driver snapped on the head-lights and the car moved onto the road.

The ride took half an hour. When the lights of a small town glowed weakly ahead, the massive car pulled from the rutted, uneven road, onto the shoulder. Among the weeds and debris the door was opened, and Jones was motioned out. The guard climbed back in wordlessly, slammed the door, and off roared the car, leaving Jones standing alone.

He began walking toward the lights of the town. Presently a partly-demolished gas station rose into view. Next came a roadside tavern, a bar, a closed-down grocery store and a drugstore. And, finally, a gigantic, crumbling hotel.

In the lobby of the hotel lounged a few men, most of them old, eyes vacant, without hope, smoking and waiting listlessly. Jones strode among them to the telephone booth beside the desk. Fishing a two-dollar piece from his pocket he rapidly dialed.

"I'm at a town called Laurel Heights," he told the individual who answered. "Come and pick me up."

After that he strolled restlessly around the lobby, gazing through the fly-specked window at the dark road beyond.

They would all be waiting, and he was impatient to begin. First came his speech and then the questions, but to him it was a formality; he had previewed long ago the grudging, reluctant acceptance of his conditions. They would protest but in the end they would give in; the publisher, first, and then General Patzech, and then Mrs. Winestock whose Montana estate provided the meeting place and whose money was to finance the Organization.

The name pleased him. They would call themselves Patriots United. Tillman, the industrialist, would suggest it; the legal arrangements had already been put through by David Sullivan, the councilman from New York. It had all been arranged, and it was going to work out as planned.

In front of the hotel appeared a slim needle-nosed projectile. Cautiously, the projectile came to rest against the curb; its lock fastened, and the hull slid back. Jones hurried from the lobby out into the night cold. Making his way to the projectile, he felt in the darkness for the opening.

"It's about time," he told the shapes half-visible in the gloom. "Are they all there?"

"Every one of them," the answer came. "All assembled and ready to listen. Got your seat-straps fastened?"

He had. The hull slid shut, snapped into place, and the lock released. An instant later the needle-nose raced forward into the sky. It headed west toward Montana and the Bitterroot Mountains; Jones was on his way.

7

On the bulletin board of the post office, among the escaped-counterfeiter notices and information on rocket mail, hung a large white square, firmly taped in place behind protective glass.

It is hereby stated by the Department of Public Health of
the Federal World Government that the migratory protozoa referred to as *drifters* are benign, incomplete single-
celled organisms incapable of affecting human safety or
property, and if left alone will succumb to the natural
temperature of the Earth's surface. It is further advised
that any person witnessing the aforedescribed mistreat-
ment of migratory protozoa referred to as *drifters* will be
rewarded with the cash sum of ten thousand Westbloc
dollars.   Oct 7 2002

Most of the escaped-counterfeiter notices and information
on rocket mail were yellowed, dog-eared, fly-specked with
age. This notice remained bright and clean throughout its
life: after it had hung for perhaps three hours, the protective
glass was carefully slid aside, and the notice removed. The
notice was torn up and thrown away. And the glass re-closed.

The man who led this particular mob had red hair and was
blind in one eye. Otherwise he looked like any other wide-
shouldered laborer striding along at the head of a
mob . . . Except that when he emerged briefly in the moon-
light, an armband was momentarily visible, and in his right
hand was gripped a portable wireless field telephone.

The mob wasn't a mob, either. It was a tightly-organized
line of dedicated men. Behind those men came a straggling,
undisciplined crowd composed of high school boys, girls in
white shorts, children wheeling bikes, middle-aged workmen,
sharp-faced housewives, dogs, and a few old people with their
arms folded against the cold. For the most part the crowd
stayed behind and minded their own business; it was the line
of dedicated men responding to the red-headed leader who
did the actual work. And the red-headed leader was carrying
out instructions relayed over the field telephone.

"The next house," the field telephone was saying, in its
odd little whisper, compounded of night and metallic cob-

webs. "I can see it pretty well. Watch your step; somebody's coming to meet you."

Overhead, the scout plane rotated its jets and secured itself directly above the quarry. The quarry had come to rest on the roof of a long-abandoned warehouse. It was virtually invisible; nobody knew how long it had lain there, drying and cracking in the hot sunlight, sweating cold drops of mist during the long nights. It had just now been detected by one of the periodic aerial flights over the town.

It was a big one.

"God," the field telephone gasped, as the scout plane gingerly lowered itself. "It's a granddaddy. It's big as a barn. Must be old as hell."

The red-headed leader didn't answer; he was cautiously scanning the side of the warehouse, looking for a ladder to the roof. Finally he made it out: a fire-escape ladder that ended ten feet from the pavement.

"Get those boxes," he ordered one of his men. "Those trash boxes over in that alley."

Two men broke away from the line; handing their flashlights to others behind them, they trotted across the silent street. It was late, well past midnight. The factory district of Omaha Falls was forbidding and deserted. Far off, a car motor sounded. Now and then somebody in the tautly-watching crowd coughed or sneezed or murmured. None of them spoke out loud; rapt, fascinated, with an almost religious awe, they watched the men drag the trash boxes over and stack them under the ladder.

A moment later the red-headed man leaped up, caught the last rung, and dragged the ladder down.

"There you go," the field telephone said, in the hands of one of his men. "Be careful when you get up on the roof . . . it's right at the edge."

"Is it alive?" the red-headed man demanded, momentarily taking back the field telephone.

"Think so. It stirred a little, but it's weak."

Satisfied, the red-headed man snatched up the ten-gallon drum of gasoline and climbed the ladder. Under his strong fingers the metal was sweaty. Grunting, he continued on, past the second floor of the warehouse, past the gaping, broken holes that had been windows. A few indistinct shapes filled the building, obsolete war machinery rusting and discarded. Now he was almost at the roof. Halting, he held on for a moment, getting his wind and examining the situation.

The lip of the roof was visible. To his nostrils came the faint pungent scent of the drifter; the odor of drying flesh that he had come to know so well. He could almost see it. With great caution he climbed one more rung; now it was clearly visible.

The drifter was the largest he had seen. It lay across the roof of the warehouse, folded and wadded in thick layers. One edge dripped loosely over the side; if he wished, he could reach out his hand and touch it. But he didn't wish. Frightened, he involuntarily pulled back. He hated even to look at them, but he had to. Sometimes, he had to touch them; and once, one dreadful time, he had slipped and fallen into one, found himself half-buried in the quivering mass of protoplasm.

"How's it look?" a man below shouted up.

"Fine."

"Is it big?"

"Very." The red-headed man poised himself expertly and craned his neck. The drifter looked old and noticeably yellow: its fluid had turned an aged opaque, discoloring the asphalt roof beneath. It was quite thin, of course; each layer was only a fraction of an inch thick. And it was alien. A foreign, unfamiliar life-form, dropped from the sky onto the roof of this warehouse. His gorge rose up in his throat and almost choked him. Turning away, he bent down and fumbled with the lid of the gasoline drum.

The gasoline had been strewn over the roof and the match applied, when the first police ship came screaming down, past the slow scout plane, directly at the roof.

The crowd scattered; the scout plane scuttled off. Standing in the safety of the shadows, the red-headed man perceived that the fire could not be put out. A police fire-ship squirted futile foam for awhile and then retired. The fire-ship hesitated, then dropped below roof-level, to halt the blaze from spreading downward. The drifter itself had already perished. Once, the drying cadaver shivered and sent flaming bits of itself showering down on the pavement. Rapidly, it curled, shriveled, oozed out its life-fluids, and degenerated. A shrill high-pitched squeal echoed up and down the street; its living sap was protesting mindlessly against the fire. Then the remaining tissue charred and disintegrated into smoking fragments. The fire-ship hoisted itself, squirted a few perfunctory times, and then retreated.

"That's it," the red-headed man said into the field telephone. He felt a deep and lasting satisfaction, knowing that he personally had killed the alien life-form. "Now we can get going."

8

On the brightly-lit stage colorful shapes danced and gestured. The costumed figures sang lustily, bustily; scenery glimmered with a high sparkle: a small square of brilliance cut in the far end of the hall. The third act was coming to an end. All the characters were on stage; with infinite precision they gave forth their melodic lines. In the pit, the orchestra—classical and exact—labored furiously.

Dominating the opera loomed the aged, wallowing figure of Gaetano Tabelli, long past his prime but still a splendid singer and actor. Purple-faced, near-sighted, the fabulous Tabelli waddled about the stage, an expression of dumbfounded bewilderment on his huge wrinkled features, struggling grotesquely to find his way through the maze of shadows that made up the world of Beaumarchais. Peering through his eye-glass, Tabelli grossly scrutinized his fellows, bellowing all the while in his vast, familiar, booming bass-baritone. A greater Don Bartolo there never was. And never would be. This performance, this zenith of consummate operatic staging, dramatic force, and perfected vocal artistry, had been frozen for all time. Tabelli was dead, now, ten years.

The bright figures on the stage were scrupulous robot imitations.

But even so, the performance was wholly convincing. Relaxed and comfortable in his deep chair, Cussick watched with passive appreciation. He enjoyed *Le Nozze di Figaro*. He had seen Tabelli many times; he had never become tired of the great performer's finest role. And he enjoyed the gay costumes, the uninterrupted flow of lyrical melody, the pink-cheeked chorus singing peasant interludes for all they were worth. The music and phantasmagoria of colors had gradually put him in a soporific state. Dreaming, half-asleep, he leaned back in his seat and happily absorbed it all.

But something was wrong.

Awakened, he pulled himself upright. Beside him, Nina sat slumped in rapt satisfaction; her mood was unbroken. Before he realized what he was doing, he had slid to his feet.

Blinking, Nina broke out of her trance. "What?" she whispered, astonished. He made a silencing motion and pushed his way down the row to the aisle. A moment later he was plodding stonily past rows of attentive faces to the carpeted steps in the rear, and the packed standing room. There he paused to take one final look at the stage.

The feeling remained, even at this distance. He stepped past the calcified ushers and reached the lobby. There, in the now empty, carpeted vault that still smelled of cigar smoke and women's perfume, he halted and lit a fresh cigarette.

He was the only person in the whole deserted lobby. Behind him, through the half-open doors, rang the sounds and voices and the sweet fluttering whirr of a Viennese symphony orchestra. Vaguely irritated, he prowled around. His restlessness remained; and it hadn't been helped by the quick glare of disapproval that had hardened on Nina's face. He had seen it before; he knew what it meant. Explanations were going to be needed. He winced at the thought.

How could he explain?

Beyond the lobby of the opera house stretched the night street, sunk in desolate stillness. On the far side were deserted office buildings, black and empty, locked up for the week-end. The entrance of one glowed; a night-light flickered dully. In the concrete well lay heaps of rubbish blown there by the night wind. Posters, scraps of paper, urban trash of various kinds. Even from where he stood, insulated by thick plate glass doors, by the descending flight of concrete steps, by the wide sidewalk and street itself, Cussick could make out the letters on a crumpled poster.

PATRIO
rally a
of the ma
JONES WILL
public invi

Torn across the middle, the poster lay sightlessly sprawled. But for every one that had been ripped down by the police, a thousand still plastered walls, doorways; hung in restaurants, store windows, bars, lavatories, gas stations, schools, offices, private houses. The Pied Piper and his flock . . . the reek of burning gasoline.

When the final thunderous roar of applause burst out, Cussick tensed himself. Already, a few eager people scurried from the open doorways; ushers appeared and rapidly fixed the doors aside. Now the first phalanx of the throng burst forth; laughing and conversing, pulling their wraps around them, the well-dressed citizens of the main floor poured into the lobby, like a jar of expensive costume jewelry abruptly overturned. Down the wide stairs, less elaborately dressed patrons descended. In a moment, Cussick was surrounded by a solid pack of talking, murmuring, noisily gesturing people.

Presently Nina fought her way over to him.

"Hello," he said uncomfortably.

"What happened?" Nina inquired, half-anxiously, half in exasperation. "Did you have some sort of fit?"

"Sorry." It was a difficult thing to explain to her. "That last act scenery reminded me of something. Dismal, like that. People creeping around in the darkness."

Lightly, Nina said: "Reminded you of business? Police prisons, maybe?" Her voice was tense, sharpened with momentary accusation. "Guilty conscience?"

He felt his face flushing. "No, that isn't it." Apparently he answered too loudly; some of the nearby people glanced curiously around. Cussick snapped his jaws angrily together and shoved his hands deep in his pockets. "Let's talk about it some other time."

"All right," Nina said brightly, smiling her familiar flash of white teeth. "No scenes—not tonight." Agilely, she spun on her heel, taking in the sight of the surrounding clusters of people. The tight line of her forehead showed she was still upset; he had no doubts about that. But the clash was going to be postponed.

"I'm sorry," Cussick repeated awkwardly. "It's this damn stuff going on. The dark stage reminded me of it. I always forget that whole scene is set at night."

"Don't worry about it," Nina answered insistently, wanting to drop the subject. Her sharp nails dug quickly into his arm. "What time is it? Is it midnight?"

He examined his wristwatch. "Somewhat after."

Frowning, Nina peered urgently toward the sidewalk outside. Taxis were sliding into the loading zone, picking up passengers and starting immediately off. "Do you think we missed him? He'd wait, wouldn't he? I thought I saw him, a second ago, as I was coming out."

"Isn't he meeting us at the apartment?" Somehow, he couldn't imagine Kaminski at a Mozart opera; the round-faced worried man with his thick mustache was from a different century entirely.

"No, dear," Nina said patiently. "He's meeting us here— remember? You were thinking about something else, as usual. We're supposed to wait for him; he doesn't know where we live."

The crowd was beginning to flow from the lobby outside onto the street. Gusts of frigid night air billowed in; coats were put on, furs slipped in place. The intimated odor of perfume and cigar smoke very soon dwindled as the remote, hostile vacuum of the outside world made its way in.

"Our little cosmos is breaking up," Cussick observed morbidly. "The real world is on its way."

"What's that?" Nina asked vacantly, still critically studying the women around them. "Look what that girl is wearing. Over there, the one in blue."

While Cussick was going through the motions of looking, a familiar figure came threading its way toward them. "Hi," Kaminski said, as he reached them. "Sorry I'm late. I forgot all about it."

The sight of Max Kaminski was a shock. He hadn't seen his one-time Political Instructor in months. Kaminski was haggard and hunched over; his eyes were bloodshot, underscored with puffy black circles. His fingers trembled as he reached out to shake hands. Under one arm he clutched a bulky brown-wrapped package. Nodding slightly to Nina, aware of her for the first time, he murmured: "Evening, Nina. Good to see you again."

"You weren't at the opera," Nina observed, with a distasteful glance at the man's rumpled business suit and the messy package.

"No, I missed it." Kaminski's hand was wet and clammy; he drew it back and stood clumsily, focussing with an effort. "I can't sit through long things. Well, are we ready to go?"

"Certainly," Nina said, in an icy voice; her dismay was fast turning to outright aversion. Kaminski had evidently been working through a fifteen-hour double shift; fatigue and nervous exhaustion were written in every pore of his stooped body. "What's that you have?" she asked, indicating the package.

"I'll show you later," Kaminski assured her noncommittally, tightening his grip.

"Let's go, then," Nina said briskly, taking her husband's arm. "Where to?"

"This girl," Kaminski muttered, shambling along after them. "We have to pick her up. You don't know her . . . I forgot to tell you about her. Very nice kid. It'll make us an even four-square." He tried to laugh, but what came out sounded more like a death-rattle. "Don't ask me to introduce her—I don't know her last name. I sort of picked her up in one of the outer offices."

Presently Nina said: "I'd like to go to the apartment, first. I want to see how Jackie is."

"Jackie?" Puzzled, Kaminski hurried down the concrete steps behind them. "Who's that?"

"Our son," Nina said distantly.

"That's right," Kaminski admitted. "You have a child. I've never seen him." His voice trailed off. . . . "With all this work, I don't know if I'm coming or going."

"Right now you're going," Nina said, standing on the curb, her body straight and disapproving, arms folded, waiting rigidly for a taxi. "Are you sure you feel up to this? It looks as if you've already had your share of celebrating."

Cussick said sharply: "Cut it."

The taxi came and Nina slipped gingerly inside. The two men followed, and the taxi shot off into the sky. Below them, the lights of Detroit sparkled and winked, evenly-spaced stars in a man-made firmament. Fresh night air swirled into the cabin of the taxi, a harsh but reviving wind that helped clear Cussick's head. Presently Kaminski seemed to recover a trifle.

"Your husband and I haven't been doing so well, lately," he told Nina: a belated apology. "You've probably noticed."

Nina nodded.

"We're falling apart. The strain . . ." He grimaced. "It isn't easy to watch everything you stand for falling apart piece by piece. One brick after another."

"The graphs still going up?" Cussick asked.

"Straight up. Every region, every stratum. He's getting through to everybody . . . a cross-section. How the hell can we isolate a thing like that? There's gasoline frying on every street corner in the world."

Nina said thoughtfully: "Does that surprise you?"

"It's illegal," Kaminski retorted, with childish venom. "They have no right to kill those things."

The woman's thin, pencilled eyebrows went up. "Do you really care about those—lumps?"

"No," Kaminski admitted. "Of course not. I wish they'd all sizzle into the sun. And neither does he; nobody cares about the drifters one way or another."

"How strange," Nina said, in a carefully modulated voice. "Millions of people are resentful, willing to break the law to show their resentment, and you say nobody cares."

"Nobody that counts," Kaminski said, losing all sense of what he was saying: "Just the dupes care, the idiots. Jones knows and we know—the drifters are a means, not an end. They're a rallying point, a pretext. We're playing a game, a big elaborate game." Wearily, he muttered: "God, I hate it."

"Then," Nina said practically, "stop playing it."

Kaminski brooded. "Maybe you're right. Sometimes I think that; times when I'm working away, buried in graphs and reports. It's an idea."

"Let them burn the drifters," Cussick said, "and then what? Is that the end of it?"

"No." Kaminski nodded reluctantly. "Of course not. Then the real business begins. Because the drifters aren't here; only a few of them are in our system. They come from somewhere; they have a point of origin."

"Beyond the dead eight," Nina said enigmatically.

Aroused from his lethargy, Kaminski pulled himself around to peer at the woman. Shrewd, wrinkled face dark with suspicion, he was still studying her when the taxi began to lower. Nina opened her purse and found a fifty-dollar bill.

"Here we are," she said shortly. "You can come inside if you want. Or you can wait here—it'll only take a second."

"I'll come inside," Kaminski said, visibly not wanting to be left alone. "I'd like to see your child . . . I've never seen him." As he fumbled for the door he muttered uncertainly: "Have I?"

"No," Cussick answered, deeply struck by his aging instructor's deterioration. Carefully, he reached past Kaminski and opened the taxi door. "Come on inside and get warm."

The living room of the apartment lit up in anticipation as Nina pushed open the front door. From the bedroom came a bubbling, aggravated wail; Jackie was awake and cross.

"Is he all right?" Cussick asked anxiously. "Isn't that thing working?"

"He's probably hungry," Nina answered, taking off her coat and tossing it over a chair. "I'll go heat up his bottle." Skirt swirling around her ankles, she disappeared down the hall into the kitchen.

"Sit down," Cussick said.

Kaminski seated himself gratefully. He laid his package down beside him on the couch. "Nice little place you have here. Clean, fresh, everything new."

"We redecorated it when we moved in."

Kaminski looked around uneasily. "Is there anything I can do to help?"

"Help?" Cussick laughed. "No, unless you're an expert in baby-feeding."

"I'm not." Unhappily, Kaminski picked at the sleeve of his coat. "Never had anything to do with that." He glanced around at the living room, a wan hunger rising to his face. "You know, I sure as hell envy you."

"This?" The living room was well-furnished and tidy. A small, rigorously-maintained apartment, showing a woman's taste in furnishings and decoration. "I suppose so," Cussick admitted. "Nina keeps it nice. But it's only four rooms." He added dryly: "As Nina occasionally reminds me."

Fretfully, Kaminski said: "Your wife feels a lot of hostility toward me. I'm sorry—it bothers me. Why does she feel that way?"

"Police."

"She resents the service?" Kaminski nodded. "I thought that was it. It's not popular, now. And it's getting less popular. As Jones goes up, we go down."

"She never did like it," Cussick said, his voice soft; he could hear the distant sounds of Nina stirring around in the kitchen, warming the baby's formula, her heels clicking as she hurried into the bedroom, faint murmurs as she talked to the baby. "She came from an information agency. Relativism never sank very deeply into the communication media; they're still tied up with the old slogans of Goodness, Truth, and Beauty. The police aren't beautiful, certainly . . . and she wonders if they're good." Sardonically, he went on: "After all, to admit the necessity of the secret police would be to admit the existence of fanatical absolutist cults."

"But she's heard about Jones."

"Sometimes I think women are totally passive receptors, like pieces of litmus paper."

"Some women." Kaminski shook his head. "Not all."

"What the public thinks of Jones she thinks. I can tell what they believe by talking to her. She seems to get it intuitively, by some sort of psychic osmosis." Presently he added: "One day she stole some little glasses from a store. I couldn't figure it out at the time. Later I understood it . . . but it took two more times to make it clear."

"Oh," Kaminski said. "Yes, of course. You're a cop. She resents you. So she breaks the law . . . she asserts herself against cops." He glanced up. "Does she understand it?"

"Not exactly. She knows she feels moral indignation at me. I like to think it's nothing but outworn slogan-idealism. But maybe it's more. Nina's ambitious; she came from a good family. Socially, she'd like to be sitting up in the boxes, not down on the main floor. Being married to a cop has never been socially useful. There's a stigma. She can't get over that."

Kaminski said thoughtfully: "You say that. But I know you're completely in love with her."

"Well, I hope I can keep her."

"Would you leave Security to keep her? If it was a choice?"

"I can't say. I hope I never have to make the choice. Probably it depends on where this Jones thing goes. And nobody can see that—except Jones."

Nina appeared in the doorway. "He's fine, now. We can go."

Rising to his feet, Cussick asked: "You feel like going out?"

"I certainly do," Nina said emphatically. "I'm not going to sit around here; I can tell you that much."

As the woman collected her things, Kaminski asked hesitantly, "Nina, could I see Jack before we leave?"

Nina smiled; her face softened. "Sure, Max. Come on in the bedroom." She put down her things. "Only don't make too much noise."

Kaminski gathered up his package and the two men obediently followed her. The bedroom was dark and warm. In his bassinet the baby lay soundly sleeping, one hand raised to his mouth, knees drawn up. Kaminski stood for a time, hands on the railing of the bassinet. The only sound was the baby's muted rasp and the continual click of the robot watcher.

"He wasn't really hungry," Nina said. "It had fed him." She indicated the watcher. "He just missed me."

Kaminski started to reach down toward the baby, then changed his mind. "He's healthy-looking," he said awkwardly. "Looks a lot like you, Doug. He has your forehead. But he's got Nina's hair."

"Yes," Cussick agreed. "He's going to have nice hair."

"What color eyes?"

"Blue. Like Nina. The perfect human being: my powerful intellect and her beauty." He put his arm around his wife and held her tight.

Chewing his lip, Kaminski said half aloud: "I wonder what the world's going to be like, when he grows up. I wonder if he'll be running through ruins with a gun and an armband . . . chanting a slogan."

Abruptly, Nina turned and left the bedroom. When they followed they found her standing at the living room door, her coat on, purse under her arm, pulling on her gloves with rapid, jerky motions.

"Ready?" she demanded, in a clipped voice. With her sharp toe she kicked open the hall door. "Then let's go. We'll pick up this *girl* of Max's, and get under way."

9

The girl was waiting demurely at the Security annex. Kaminski ordered the taxi to pull up at the darkened runway; he leaped out and strode up the gloomy walk, toward the long concrete building. After a short interval he returned with a small, solemn figure. By now he had managed to get her name.

"Tyler," he muttered, helping her into the taxi, "this is Doug and Nina Cussick." Indicating the girl, he finished: "Tyler Fleming."

"Hello," Tyler said huskily, tossing her head back and smiling shyly around at them. She had large dark eyes and short-cropped jet-black hair. Her skin was smooth and faintly tanned. She was slender, almost thin, body very young and unformed under her simple evening dress.

Nina examined her critically and said: "I've seen you around. Aren't you a Security employee?"

"I'm in research," Tyler answered, in an almost inaudible whisper. "I've only been with Security a few months."

"You'll get along," Nina observed, signalling the taxi to rise. In a moment they were on their way up. Irritably, Nina stabbed down on the high-velocity stud mounted by her armrest. "It's almost one o'clock," she explained. "If we don't hurry, we won't see anything."

"See?" Cussick echoed apprehensively.

At Nina's direction, the taxi let them off in the North-beach section of San Francisco. Cussick satisfied the robot meter with ninety dollars in change, and the taxi shot off. To their right was Columbus Avenue and its notorious rows of bars and dives and cabarets and blackmarket restaurants. People were out roaming the streets in great numbers; the sky overhead was choked with inter-city taxis setting down and taking off. Multicolored signs winked; on every side glared chattering, flickering displays.

Seeing where Nina had brought them, Cussick felt a pang of dismay. He knew she had been going to San Francisco; police reports had mentioned her presence in the Northbeach surveillance area. But he had assumed it was clandestine, a covert protest; he hadn't expected her to bring him along. Nina was already heading purposefully toward the descend-ing stairs of a subsurface bar; she seemed to know exactly where she was going.

Catching up with her, he demanded: "You sure you want to do this?"

Nina halted. "Do what?"

"This is one area I wish they had demolished. Too bad the bombs didn't finish it once and for all."

"We'll be all right," she assured him primly. "I know peo-ple here."

"My God," Kaminski exclaimed, seeing for the first time where they were. "We're close to *them!*"

"To whom?" Cussick asked, puzzled.

Kaminski's sagging face snapped oblique. He said nothing more; placing his hand on Tyler's shoulder, he guided her toward the stairs. Nina had already started down; reluctantly, Cussick followed after her. Kaminski came last, in a dark world of his own, thinking and muttering about esoteric matters known only in the gnawing doubt of his own consciousness. Tyler, serious and sedate, descended willingly, without resistance. Young as she was, she seemed totally self-possessed; there was no sign of wonder on her face.

The underground level was jammed with people, a densely-packed mass that stirred and undulated like a single organism. A constant blare of tinny noise roared up deafeningly; the air was transluscent with a shimmer of smoke, perspiration, and the steady shouting of human beings. Robot servants, suspended from the ceiling, wheeled here and there, serving drinks and collecting glasses.

"Over here," Nina called, leading the way. Cussick and Kaminski exchanged glances; these places were not strictly illegal, of course, but Security would have preferred to close them. The San Francisco Northbeach region was the bête noire of the vice squads, a last remnant of the prewar red-light stratum.

Nina seated herself at a tiny wooden table crammed against the wall. Overhead, an imitation candle flickered fitfully. Cussick pulled up a packing crate and settled himself uncomfortably; Kaminski went through the mechanical ritual of finding Tyler a chair, and then one for himself. Bending over, he laid his package on the floor, propped against a table leg. The four people sat pressed tightly together, elbows and feet touching, facing one another across the square water-logged surface of the table.

"Well," Nina said gaily, "here we are."

Her voice was barely audible above the din. Cussick hunched over and tried to shut out the constant clamor. The close air, the frenetic motion of people, made him vaguely ill. Nina's good time had a grim, deliberate quality about it; he wondered what Tyler thought. She didn't seem to think anything; pretty, competent, she sat unfastening her coat, an agreeable expression on her face.

"This is the price we pay," Kaminski's voice came in Cussick's ear. "We have Relativism; everybody to his own tastes."

Some of his words reached Nina. "Oh yes," she agreed, with a tight smile. "You have to let people do as they want."

The robot waiter dropped like a metal spider from the ceiling, and Nina turned her attention to ordering. From the bill-of-fare she selected an oral preparation of heroin, then passed the punch sheet to her husband.

Petrified, Cussick watched the robot bring forth a cellophane packet of white capsules. "You're taking those?" he demanded.

"Now and then," Nina answered noncommittally, tearing open the packet with her sharp nails.

Numbly, Cussick ordered marijuana for himself; Kaminski did the same. Tyler examined the bill-of-fare with interest, and finally chose a liqueur built around the drug *artemisia*. Cussick paid the bill, and the waiter, after delivering the orders, accepted the money and sailed off.

His wife, already under the influence of the heroin, sat glassy-eyed, breathing shallowly, hands clenched together. A faint sheen of perspiration had risen to her throat; drop by drop it trickled down to her collarbone and evaporated in the warmth of the room. The drug, he knew, had been severely cut by police order; but it was still a powerful narcotic. He could sense an almost invisible rhythmic motion to her body; she was swaying back and forth to some auditory disturbance unheard by others.

Reaching out, he touched her hand. Her flesh was cold, hard, as pale as stone. "Darling," he said gently.

With an effort, she was able to focus on him. "Hi," she said, a little sadly. "How are you?"

"Do you really hate us this much?"

She smiled. "Not you, us. All of us."

"Why?"

"Well," Nina said, in a remote, detached voice, brought

down to reality by fantastic concentration of will, "it just seems so goddamn hopeless. Everything . . . like Max says. There's nothing. We're living in deadness."

Kaminski, pretending not to hear, pretending not to listen, sat frozen, taking in every word, responding with intense pain.

"I mean," Nina said, "there was the war, and now here we are. And Jackie, too. For what? Where can we go? What can we look for? We're not even allowed to have romantic illusions, anymore. We can't even tell ourselves lies. If we do—" She smiled, without rancor. "Then they take us to the forced labor camps."

It was Kaminski who answered. "We have Jones . . . The Whirlwind, sweeping us away. That's the worst thing about our world . . . it's permitted the beast to come."

Tyler sipped her cocktail and said nothing.

"What now?" Nina asked. "You can't keep your world going . . . you realize it's finished. Jones has come. You have to recognize him. He's the future; it's all interwoven, tied-up, mixed. You can't have one without the other . . . your world has no future of its own."

"Jones will kill us all," Kaminski said.

"But at least it'll have meaning. We'll be doing something." Nina's voice trailed off, moving farther away from them. "It'll be *for* something. We'll be reaching out, like we used to."

"Empty idealism," Cussick said unhappily.

Nina didn't answer. She had disappeared into an inner world; her face was blank, devoid of personality.

On the raised platform at the rear of the room a commotion had begun swinging into life. The floor show of the place: the nightly spectacle. Patrons turned their attention to it; the clog of people at the foot of the stairs craned their necks eagerly. Listlessly, Cussick watched, indifferent to what was happening, his hand still resting on his wife's.

The floor show involved two figures, a man and a woman.

They smiled at the audience, and then removed their clothing. Cussick was reminded of the first day he had seen Jones, that day in early spring, when he had tramped across the slushy black ground to visit the carnival. The bright April day he had witnessed the assorted sports and freaks and mutants collected from the war. Recollection welled up inside him, a mixed nostalgia for his own hopeful youth, his vague ambitions and idealism.

The two figures on the stage, professionally agile and supple-bodied, had begun making love. The action was carried out as a ritual: it had been done so many times that it was a series of dance-motions, without passion or intensity. Presently, as a kind of mounting tempo, the sex of the man began to change. After a time it was the rhythmic motions of two women. Then, toward the conclusion, the figure that had originally presented itself as a woman transformed itself to a man. And the dance ended as it had begun: with a man and a woman quietly making love.

"Quite a feat," Kaminski admitted, as the man and woman put on their clothing, bowed, and left the stage. They had exchanged clothes: the final effect was overwhelming. A round of sincere applause rippled through the room: the couple were artists. "I remember when I first saw hermaphrodite mutants in action. Now it seems just one more"— Kaminski searched ironically—"One more example of Relativism in action."

For awhile none of the four people spoke. Finally Tyler said: "I wonder how far we can go."

"I think we've gone as far as we can," Cussick answered. "All we can hope for now is to hang on."

"Did we go too far?" Kaminski asked, appealingly.

"No," Cussick said flatly. "We were right. We're right now. It's a paradox, a contradiction, a criminal offense to say it. *But we're right*. Secretly, covertly, we've got to believe it." His fingers clutched convulsively around his wife's cold hand.

"We've got to try to keep our world from falling completely apart."

"Maybe it's too late," Kaminski said.

"Yes," Nina agreed suddenly. "It's too late." Her fingers jerked away from Cussick's. Jaw working spasmodically, she hunched forward, teeth chattering, pupils dilated. "Please, darling—"

Cussick rose, and Tyler beside him. "I'll take care of her," Tyler said, moving around the table to Nina. "Where's the women's room?"

"Thanks," Kaminski said, accepting a cigarette from Cussick. The women had not returned. As he lit up, Kaminski remarked: "I suppose you know Jones has written a book."

"Different from the Patriots United publications?"

From the floor by the table Kaminski lifted up his brown-wrapped package; he untied it carefully. "This is a summary. *The Moral Struggle* it's called. It outlines his whole program: what he really wants, what he really stands for. The mythos of the movement." He set the bulky volume down in the center of the table and riffled the pages.

"Have you read this?" Cussick asked, examining it.

"Not the whole thing. It isn't complete; Jones is pontificating it orally. The book is transcribed from his harangues . . . it's growing by leaps and bounds."

"What did you mean," Cussick asked, "when you said we were near *them?* Who were you talking about?"

A strange, oblique, withdrawn look appeared on the older man's face. Gathering up his book, he began to rewrap it. "I don't remember saying that.

"As we were coming in."

Kaminski fooled with his package; he laid it back on the floor, against the table-leg. "One of these days you may be brought into it. But not yet."

"Can you give me any information?"

"No, not really. It's been going on awhile; it's important. Obviously, it's here in this area. Obviously, it involves a number of individuals."

"Does Jones know?"

Kaminski shuddered. "God forbid. Sure, maybe. Doesn't he know everything? Anyhow, he can't do anything about it . . . he has no legal power."

"Then this is under Fedgov."

"Oh, yes," Kaminski agreed bleakly. "Fedgov is still in business. Trying out a few last tricks before it goes down to ruin."

"You don't sound like you think we can beat this thing."

"Do I sound like that? All we're up against is a prophet . . . we ought to be able to handle that. There've been prophets before; the New Testament is full of them."

"What do you mean by that? There's John the Baptist; you mean him?"

"I mean Him Who John foretold."

"You're raving."

"No, I'm repeating. I hear that kind of stuff. The Second Coming . . . after all, He *was* supposed to show up again, sometime. And the world certainly needs him, now."

"But that puts the drifters in the position of—" Cussick grimaced. "What's the term?"

"Hordes from Hell." Blowing clouds of gray cigarette smoke, Kaminski continued: "Satan's Legions. The Evil Ones."

"Then we haven't gone back a hundred years. We've gone back a thousand."

"Maybe this won't be so bad. The drifters aren't people; they're mindless blobs. Let's assume the worst: let's assume Jones gets a war whipped up. We finish the drifters here, and then clean the planets one by one. After that—" Kaminski gestured. "To the stars. With bulging battleships. Hunting down the bastards, exterminating the race. Well? What then?

The enemy's gone; a race of gigantic amoebae has perished. *Is that so bad?* I'm only trying to see the possibilities in this. We'll be out beyond the system. And right now, without the spur, the hatred, the sense of fighting an enemy, we just sit around."

"You're saying what Jones says," Cussick reflected.

"You bet I am."

"Want me to show you your error? The danger isn't in the war; it's in the attitude that makes the war possible. To fight, we have to believe we're Right and they're Wrong. White versus black—good versus evil. The drifters have nothing to do with it; they're only a means."

"I'd disagree with you on one point," Kaminski said intently. "You're convinced, are you, that in the war itself there's no danger?"

"Sure," Cussick said. But he was suddenly uncertain. "What can primitive, one-celled protoplasm do to us?"

"I don't know. But we've never fought a war with nonterrestrials. I wouldn't want to take the chance. Remember, we still don't know what they are. We may be surprised one of these days. Surprised or even worse. We may find out."

Threading their way among the tightly-packed tables, Tyler and Nina returned to their seats. Pale and shaken, but fully in command of herself, Nina sat clasping her hands together, her attention on the raised platform. "Are they gone?" she asked faintly.

"We were wondering," Tyler said, "how those hermaphrodites decide. That is, while Nina and I were in there, one of them might come in, too, and we wouldn't know whether to resent it." Daintily, she sipped at her drink. "A lot of unusual-looking women came and went, but neither one of the hermaphrodites."

"There's one of them over there," Nina said shakily. "Over by the tune-maker."

Leaning against the square metal machine stood one of

the dancers, the one that had originated as a young man. It was still a woman, as it had ended its act. Slender, with close-cut sandy hair, wearing a skirt and blouse and sandals, it was a perfect androgyne. Its smooth, neutral face was empty of expression; it looked a trifle tired, nothing more.

"Ask her to come over," Nina said, touching her husband's arm.

"There's no room," Cussick said flatly; he didn't want to have anything to do with it. "And don't you go over." He saw her sink back. "You stay here."

Nina flashed him a swift, animal-like glance and then subsided. "You're still feeling that way, are you?"

"What way?"

"Let it go." Nina's hands moved restlessly on the surface of the table. "Could we have something to drink? I'd like cognac."

When their fresh drinks arrived, Nina lifted her glass in a toast. "Here's to," she announced. The other glasses came up; there was a faint clink as they touched. "To a better world."

"God," Kaminski said wearily, "I hate talk like that."

Faintly amused, Nina asked: "Why?"

"Because it doesn't mean anything." Slumped over, Kaminski struggled with his whiskey sour. "Who isn't for a better world?"

"Is it true," Tyler said, after a time, "that they've sent out scouts to Proxima Centaurus?"

Kaminski nodded. "They have."

"Any luck?"

"The data hasn't been sifted."

"In other words," Tyler said, "nothing of value."

Kaminski shrugged. "Who knows?"

"Jones," Nina murmured.

"Then ask him. Or wait for the official release. Don't bother me about it."

"What's this business with Pearson?" Cussick asked, to change the subject. "I've heard rumors that he's working night and day, lining up men, organizing projects."

"Pearson is determined to stop Jones," Kaminski answered remotely. "He's sure it can be done."

"But if we get as fanatic as they are—"

"Pearson is worse. He eats, sleeps, thinks, lives Jones. He can't rest. Every time I go into his wing there's a battalion of weapons-cops hanging around: guns and tanks and projectiles."

"You think it'll do any good?"

"Darling," Nina said, measuring her words, "don't you see anything positive in it?"

"Like what?"

"I mean, here we have a man with this wonderful talent . . . he can do something we've never done. We don't have to guess anymore. *We know.* We can be sure where we're going."

"I like to guess," Cussick said flatly.

"Do you? Maybe that's where the fault lies . . . maybe you don't realize that most people want certainty. You've rejected Jones. Why? Because your system, your government, is built around not-knowing, around guesswork. It assumes nobody can know." She raised her cold blue eyes. "But now we can know. So in a way, you're outmoded."

"Well," Tyler said, amused, "then I'm out of a job."

"What did you do before you came to Security?" Cussick asked her.

"I didn't do anything: this is my first job. I'm only seventeen. I feel a little out of place with you people . . . I really don't have any experience."

Indicating the girl's glass, Kaminski said: "I can tell you one thing: that wormwood'll rot your nervous system away. It attacks the upper spinal ganglia."

"Oh, no," Tyler said quickly. "I'm doped against it." She

touched her purse. "For this, I have to depend on a synthetic neutralizer. Or I wouldn't want to take it."

Cussick's respect for her rose another notch. "What part of the world do you come from?" he asked curiously.

"I was born in China. My father was a policy-level official in the Kweiping secretariat of the Chinese People's Communist Party."

"Then you were born on that side of the war," Cussick said, amazed. "You grew up on"—he grimaced—"what people used to call the Jewish-atheist-Communist side."

"My father was a devout Party-worker. He fought with all his soul and heart against the Mohammedans and the Christian fanatics. He brought me up; my mother was killed by bacterial toxins. Since she wasn't an official, she wasn't entitled to shelter. I lived with my father in the Party offices, a mile or so underground. We were there until the war ended." She corrected herself: "That is, I was there. My father was shot by the Party near the end of the war."

"Shot for what?"

"Deviationism. The Hoff book was being circulated in our area, too. My father and I set up portions by hand . . . we circulated them among Party workers. It was quite revolutionary; many of us had never heard of the multiple-value system. The idea that everybody might be right, that everybody was entitled to his own way of life, had a startling effect on us. The Hoff concept of personal style of living . . . it was exciting. Neither religious dogma nor anti-religious dogma; no more wrangling over which interpretation of the sacred texts was correct. No more sects, splinter groups, factions; no more heretics to shoot and burn and lock up."

"You're not Chinese," Nina said.

"No, I'm English. My family were Anglican missionaries before they became Communists. There was a community of English Communists living in China."

"Do you remember much about the war?" Kaminski asked her.

"Not much. The Christian raiding parties from Formosa . . . mostly just the printing at night. The secret distribution."

"How did you get off?" Cussick asked. "Why didn't they shoot you, too?"

"I was eight years old—too young to shoot. One of the Party chiefs adopted me, a very kind old Chinese gentleman who still read Laotze and had gold carvings cut into his teeth. I was a ward of the CP when the war ended and the Party apparatus disintegrated." She shook her head. "It was all such a terrible waste . . . the war could so easily have been avoided. If people had only been just a little less fanatic."

Nina had gotten to her feet. "Darling," she said to her husband, "please, could you do me a favor? I'd like to dance."

One section of the crowded floor had been cleared for dancing; a few couples pushed mechanically back and forth. "You really feel like it?" Cussick asked warily, as he got to his feet. "Maybe for a minute."

"She's a lovely girl," Nina said distantly, as the two of them found their way out onto the packed floor.

"It's interesting, her circulating Hoff's material among Party officials."

Suddenly Nina clutched her husband tight. "I wish—" Her voice broke achingly. "Isn't there some way we can go back?"

"Back?" He was perplexed. "Back where?"

"The way we were. Not quarreling all the time. We seem to be so far apart. We don't understand each other anymore."

He held his wife close to him; under his hands her body was surprisingly fragile. "It's this damn thing . . . someday it'll be over, and we'll be together like we used to."

Stricken, Nina gazed up imploringly. "Does it have to be

over? Does it have to be gotten rid of? Can't we accept it?"

"No," Cussick said. "I'll never accept it."

The woman's sharp nails dug futilely into his back. For an interval she rested her head against his shoulder, tumble of blonde hair billowing into his face. The familiar scent of her tickled his nose: the sweet perfume of her body, the warmth of her hair. All this, the smoothness of her bare shoulders, the silky texture of her dress, the faint sheen of perspiration glowing on her upper lip. Harshly, he held her against him, squeezing her silently, yearningly. Presently she uptilted her chin, smiled waveringly, and kissed him on the mouth.

"We'll try," she said softly. "We'll do our best. Right?"

"Sure," he answered, meaning it with all his heart. "It's too important—we can't let our lives slip away like this. And now that we have Jack—" Roughly, his fingers crumpled into the base of her neck, lifting her torrent of thick hair. "We don't want to leave him for the vultures."

10

After the dance he led her back to the table, gripping her small fingers tightly until both of them had taken their seats. Kaminski sat slumped over, half-asleep, muttering vague hoarse sounds. Tyler sat trimly upright; she had finished her drink and ordered another.

"Another round?" Nina asked, with wan cheerfulness. She got hold of the waiter and reordered. "Max, you look like you're going to die on us."

With an effort, Kaminski raised his shaggy head. "Madame," he answered, "leave a man something."

The evening was coming to a close; people were beginning to filter out of the bar, back up the stairs to the street level. On the raised platform the man and woman had reappeared, removed their clothing, and once more were going through their dance. Cussick scarcely noticed them; sinking into gloomy contemplation, he sat dully sipping his drink, distantly aware of the murmur of voices, the thick opaqueness of the air. When the floor show ended, the major bulk of the audience got up and began pushing toward the exit. Already, the room was half-empty. From the street stairs a blast of frigid early-morning air swirled down, chilling the people still sitting at their tables.

"It's late," Cussick said.

Across from him, Nina's face flitted with panic. "They're not closing for a long time," she protested pathetically. "And in the back they don't close at all. Dance with me again, before we go."

Cussick shook his head. "Sorry, honey. I'd fall over."

Nina was on her feet. "Max, will you dance with me?"

"Sure," Kaminski said. "I'll do anything. Enjoy ourselves in the time left." Holding her clumsily by the arm, he half-led, half-dragged her through the departing people, to the front of the room. There, a few sodden couples swayed back and forth. The two hermaphrodites, now both women, were dancing calmly with male patrons. Presently, tired of that, they switched sexes, became men, and wandered among the tables looking for female partners.

Sitting at his table, Cussick said: "Can they control it?"

Tyler sipped her drink. "Probably. It's quite an art."

"It's depraved."

One by one the lights dimmed out. When next Cussick looked he saw Kaminski slumped over at a table, no longer dancing. Where, then, was Nina? For a time he couldn't locate her; then he identified her familiar blonde hair. She was dancing with one of the hermaphrodites, face glazed with desperate excitement. Arm around her, the slender young man danced dispassionately, expertly.

Before Cussick knew it, he was on his feet. "Wait here," he told Tyler.

Gathering up her purse and coat, Tyler started after him. "We better not get separated."

But Cussick could think only of Nina. His wife and the hermaphrodite were walking hand-in-hand through what instinct told him was the entrance to the still-functioning back rooms. Pushing a group of loitering couples aside, he followed. For an instant he waded through a dense darkness and then he was standing in a deserted corridor. Head down, he ran blindly forward. Around a turn, he stopped short.

Nina, leaning against the wall, a glass in her hand, was talking intently to the hermaphrodite. Her blonde hair was a disarranged cascade. Her body slumped with fatigue, but her eyes still flashed, bright and feverish.

Striding up to her, Cussick said: "Come on, honey. We have to go." He was dimly aware that Tyler and Kaminski had followed him.

"You go ahead," Nina said, in a strained, metallic voice. "Go on. Take off."

"What about you?" he demanded, shocked. "What about Jack?"

"The hell with Jack," she said, in sudden agony. "The hell with everything—with your whole world. I'm not going back— I'm staying here. If you want me, for God's sake *stay with me.*"

The hermaphrodite turned slightly and said to Cussick: "Mind your own business, chum. In this world, everybody does what he wants."

Cussick reached out, grabbed hold of the creature's shirt, and lifted him from his feet. The hermaphrodite was amazingly light; he struggled and twisted, and in an instant had slid out of Cussick's hands. Stepping back, the hermaphrodite flowed into a female. Her eyes mocking, she danced lithely away from him.

"Go ahead," she gasped. "Hit me."

Nina had turned and started off down the corridor. The hermaphrodite, noticing, quickly hurried after her, an eager expression on her face. As the creature followed Nina down the hall to a side door, Tyler slipped up close and caught hold of her. With an expert motion, Tyler twisted the creature around and yanked her arm back in a paralyzing lock. The hermaphrodite instantly flowed into the figure of a man. Cussick stepped forward and socked him on the jaw. Without a sound, the hermaphrodite sank down, totally unconscious, and Tyler released him.

"She's gone," Kaminski said, balancing himself with an effort. Other people were hurrying up; the hermaphrodite's partner appeared, clapped his hands in horror, and dropped down fearfully to paw at his inert companion.

Glancing around, Tyler said rapidly to Cussick: "She's familiar with this place. If you expect her to leave with you, you'll have to *talk* her into it." Urgently, she gave him a shove. "Get going."

He found her almost at once. She had crept from the corridor into a side room, a blind alley with only one entrance. There, he cornered her, slammed the door and locked it after him. Nina crouched in the corner, frail and pitiful, eyes bright with fear, trembling and gazing mutely up at him.

The room was simple, hygienically clean in its ascetic purity. The curtains, the position of the furniture, told him the unbearable truth; only Nina could have arranged this room. This was her room. Her imprint, her image, was stamped on every inch of it.

There were noises outside. Kaminski's hoarse growl swelled up: "Doug, you in there?"

He stepped outside into the hall and confronted Kaminski and Tyler. "I found her. She's all right."

"What are you going to do?" Tyler asked.

"Stay here. You two better go. Can you find your way out?"

"Certainly," Tyler said, understanding. Taking hold of Kaminski she led him back a step. "Good luck. Come on, Max. There's nothing we can do here."

"Thanks," Cussick said, standing firmly-planted in front of the door. "I'll see you later, both of you."

Kaminski, protesting and bewildered, retreated at the insistence of the slim girl holding tightly to his arm. "Give me a call," he mumbled. "When you get back; when you're out of here. So I'll know you're okay."

"I'll do that," Cussick said. "Don't forget your package." He stood a moment, until the two of them had disappeared along the hall. Then he turned and re-entered the room.

On the bed, Nina was sitting up slightly, her head against the wall, legs drawn up, feet tucked under her. She smiled up weakly at him. "Hello," she said.

"Feel better?" He locked the door and came toward her. "They left; I sent them off."

Sitting down on the edge of the bed he asked: "This is your room, isn't it?"

"Yes." She didn't look directly at him.

"How long?"

"Oh, not long. A week, maybe. Ten days."

"I don't really understand. You want to be here with these people?"

"I wanted to get away. I couldn't stand that damn little apartment . . . I wanted to be on my own, do something. It's so hard to explain; some of it I don't understand, myself. It's like the stealing—I just felt I had to stand up."

"That's why you brought us all here, then. It meant nothing until you could show it to us."

"I suppose so. Yes, I guess you're right. I wanted you to see it, so you'd know. So you'd see I had somewhere to go . . . not dependent on you. Not helpless, tied to your world. Outside in the main bar I got scared . . . I took the heroin to get my nerve." She smiled a little. "It's such a mess."

He bent over her, holding onto her hands. Her skin was cold and faintly moist. "You're not scared now, are you?"

"No," she managed. "Not with you here."

"We'll stay here tonight," he told her. "That's what you want?"

She nodded forlornly.

"Then tomorrow morning we'll go back?"

Twisting, she answered painfully: "Don't ask me. Don't make me say. I'm afraid to say, now."

"All right." It hurt, but he didn't press for an answer. "We can decide tomorrow, after we have a good sleep and breakfast. After we get all this stuff out of our systems. This poison—this rot."

There was no answer. Nina had fallen into a partial doze; eyes shut, she lay resting against the wall, chin down, body relaxed.

For a long time Cussick sat immobile. The room grew cold. Outside, in the hall, there was only silence. His watch told him it was four-thirty. Presently he bent down and slid off Nina's shoes. He placed them on the floor by the bed, hesitated, and then unfastened the snaps of her dress. The dress was intricately held together; it took him some time. Twice, she woke slightly, stirred, and sank back into sleep. At last the dress came apart; he maneuvered one section over her head, laid it over the back of a chair, lifted her hips, and struggled the remaining part away from her.

It was surprising how really small she was. Without the ornate, expensive dress, she seemed unusually bare, defenseless, open to injury. It was impossible to feel rancor toward her. He pulled up the blankets around her shoulders and tucked them under her chin. Her heavy blonde hair spilled out over the wool fabric, thick honey streaks against the checkered pattern of red and black. Smoothing her hair back from her eyes, he seated himself beside her on the bed.

For an endless time he sat, his mind blank, gazing into the shadows of the room. Nina slept fitfully; now and then she turned, twisted, made faint unhappy sounds. Struggling in an invisible darkness, she fought lonely battles, without him, without anybody. In the final analysis, each of them was cut off from the other. Each of them suffered alone.

Towards morning, he became aware of a distant, muffled sound: a noise coming from a long way off. For a time he paid no attention; the noise beat uselessly against his dulled consciousness. And then, finally, he identified it. A human voice, harsh and loud, a voice he recognized. Stiffly, shaking with cold, he got up from the bed and made his way to the door. With infinite care he unlocked it and stepped out into the chill, deserted corridor.

The voice was the voice of Jones.

Cussick walked slowly down the corridor. He passed closed doors and side passages, but saw nobody. It was five-forty A.M.; the sun was beginning to show. Through an open window at the end of the hall he caught a glimpse of bleak, gray sky, as remote and hostile as gun-metal. As he walked, the voice grew louder. All at once he turned a corner and found himself facing a great storeroom.

It wasn't Jones, not really. It was a tape recording. But the presence, the vital, cruel spirit, was there. In rows of chairs, men and women sat intently listening. The storeroom was filled with bales, boxes, huge packages heaped everywhere. The corridor had carried him to a totally different building; it linked various establishments, a variety of businesses. This was the loading stage of a commercial house.

On the wall were plastered posters. As he stood in the doorway listening to the furious, impassioned voice, he realized that this was an official meeting hall. This was a before-dawn gathering; these were working people, coming together before their work-day began. At the far end, where the speakers blared, hung Jones' emblem, the crossed flasks of Hermes. Scattered through the groups were various uniforms of the Patriots United organizations: both the women's and youth groups, armbands, badges and insignia. In a corner lounged two helmeted Security police: the meeting was no secret. The meetings were never secret: there was no necessity.

Nobody interfered with Cussick as he made his way back up the corridor. Now the building was beginning to stir; outside, rumbling commercial trucks were beginning to load and unload. He found Nina's room and entered.

She was awake. As he turned from the door she sat up, eyes wide. "Where did you go? I thought—"

"I'm back. I heard sounds." The distant snarl of Jones' voice was still audible. "That."

"Oh." She nodded. "Yes, they're meeting. That's part of this. My room."

"You've been working for them, haven't you?"

"Nothing important. Just folding papers and writing addresses. The sort of thing I used to do. Giving out information. Publicity, I guess you'd call it."

Sitting down on the edge of the bed, Cussick picked up his wife's purse and opened it. Papers, cards, lipstick, a mirror, keys, money, a handkerchief . . . he poured everything out onto the bed. Nina watched quietly; she had pulled herself up to sit leaning on one bare elbow. Cussick pawed through the contents of the purse until he came to what he wanted. "I was curious," he said. "The specific grade and date."

Her membership card in Patriots United was dated February 17, 2002. She had been a member for eight months, since before Jack was born. Code symbols with which he was familiar identified her as a full-time worker, at a fairly responsible level.

"You're really involved in this," he commented, shoveling the contents back into the purse. "While I've been busy, you've been busy, too."

"There's a lot of work," she agreed faintly. "And they need money. I've been able to help there, too. What time is it? It's about six, isn't it?"

"Not quite." He lit a cigarette and sat smoking. Amazingly, he was collected and rational. He was conscious of no emotion. Maybe it would come later. Maybe not. "Well?" he said. "I suppose it's too early to leave here."

"I'd like to sleep some more." Her eyelids drooped; she yawned, stretched, smiled at him hopefully. "Could we?"

"Sure." He stubbed out his cigarette and began unlacing his shoes.

"It's sort of exciting," Nina said wistfully. "Like an adventure—the two of us here, the locked door, the secrecy. Don't you agree? I mean, it's not—stale. Routine." As he stood by the bed unbuttoning his shirt, she went on: "I get so bored, so darn tired of the same thing, day after day. The drab ordinary life; a married woman with a baby, a frowsy housewife. It's not worth living . . . don't you feel that? Don't you want to do something?"

"I have my work."

Saddened, she answered: "I know."

He clicked off the light and approached her. White, cold sunlight filtered into the darkened room, past the edges of the window shade. In the stark luminosity, his wife's body was clearly-etched. She pushed the covers aside for him; at some time or other she had taken off the rest of her clothes, got out of bed and neatly hung her dress up in the closet. Her shoes, her stockings, her underclothes were gone, probably into dresser drawers. Moving aside for him, Nina reached out hungrily, arms avid, demanding.

"Do you think," she said tensely, "this will be the last time?"

"I don't know." He was conscious only of fatigue; gratefully, he eased himself down onto the bed, hard and narrow as it was. Nina covered him over, smoothed the wool blankets tenderly down around him. "This is your little private bed?" he asked, with a trace of irony.

"It's sort of—like in the Middle Ages," she answered.

"Just this little room, just the single bed—like a cot. The dresser and wash stand. Chastity, poverty, obedience . . . a sort of spiritual cleansing, for me. For all of us."

Cussick didn't try to think about it. The sensual, orgiastic vice of the earlier evening, the drugs and liquor and floor show, the degenerate spectacle—and now this. It made no sense. But there was a pattern, a meaning beyond logic. It fitted.

Pale shoulders, bare and lovely, pressed tight against his. Her lips parted, eyes large, Nina gazed up at him, suffused with the melting closeness of love. "Yes," she whispered, searching his face, trying to see into him, seeking to understand what he thought and felt. "I love you so damn much."

He said nothing. He touched his lips to the burning torrent of honey-flaming hair that spilled out onto the pillow and blankets. Again and again she clutched at him, clung mutely to him, tried to hold onto him. But he was already slipping away. He turned on his side, remained for a time, his hand on her throat, by her ear, fingers touching her.

"Please," Nina whispered fiercely. "Please don't leave me."

But there was nothing he could do. He was slipping further and further away from her . . . and she was leaving him, too. Locked in each other's arms, bare bodies pressed together, they were already a universe apart. Separated by the ceaseless muffled metallic drumming of the man's voice that beat against the walls from a long way off, the never-ending harsh mutter of words, gestures, speeches. The untiring din of an impassioned man.

11

The news went the rounds. Cussick didn't have to tell anybody; they all knew. It was only a month later, in the middle of November, when Tyler called him—unexpectedly, without advance warning. He was at his desk, surrounded by reports and incoming data. The call came by routine interoffice vidphone, so he wasn't prepared for it.

"Sorry to bother you," Tyler's animated image said, without preamble. She was at her desk, too; past her small, uniformed figure rested an electric typewriter and a neatly-organized office. Dark eyes large and serious, she held up a data tape that had been processed to her. "I see that your wife is being reclassified under her maiden name. We're supposed to identify her as Nina Longstren."

"That's right," Cussick agreed.

"Do you want to tell me what happened? I haven't seen you since that night."

"I'll meet you somewhere after work," he told her. "Wherever you want. But I can't talk now." He pointed to the mountain of work heaped on his desk. "I know I don't have to explain."

He met her on the wide front steps of the main Security

building. It was seven o'clock in the evening; the chill winter sky was pitch-black. In a heavy fur-lined coat, Tyler stood waiting for him, hands deep in her pockets, a wool kerchief tied around her short black hair. As he came down the concrete steps toward her, she emerged from the shadows, a cloud of moist breath hovering like a halo around her, icy particles glittering on the fur collar of her coat.

"You can tell me as little or as much as you want," she said. "I don't want you to think I'm prying."

There wasn't much to tell. At eleven the next morning he had taken Nina home to the apartment. Neither of them said more than a few words. It wasn't until he had led her into the familiar living room that both of them realized how totally futile it was. Three days later he received the preliminary notification from the marriage bureau: Nina had instigated the process of dissolution. He saw her briefly, now and then, as she collected her possessions and cleared out of the apartment. By the time the final papers had been served, she had already set up separate living quarters.

"What was your relationship?" Tyler asked. "You were still friendly, weren't you?"

That had been the miserable part. "Yes," he said tightly. "We were still friendly." He had taken Nina out to dinner on the last legal night of their marriage. The unsigned final paper had been folded up in his pocket. After listlessly sitting for an hour in the half-deserted restaurant, they had finally pushed the silverware aside and signed the papers. That was it: the marriage was over. He had taken her to a hotel, got her immediate luggage from the apartment, and left her there. The hotel idea was an elaborate charade: both of them agreed it would be better if he didn't approach her new living quarters.

"What about Jack?" Tyler asked. She shivered and blew cloudy breath toward him. "What becomes of him?"

"Jack has been entered in a Fedgov nursery. Legally, he

remains our son, but for all practical purposes we have no claim over him. We can see him when we want. But he's not responsible to us."

"Can you ever get him out? I don't know the law on those things."

"We can get him out only by joint petition." He added: "In other words, by remarrying."

"So now you're alone," Tyler said.

"That's right. Now I'm alone."

After he left Tyler, he got his car from the police lot and drove across town to the apartment. He passed seemingly endless mobs of Jones supporters—Jones Boys, as they had come to be called. At every opportunity, the organization turned out to demonstrate its growing strength. Marchers, all gripping signs, hurried through the twilight; hordes of identically-clad figures, faces rapt and devout.

> END THE TYRANNICAL REIGN
> OF ALIEN RELATIVISM
> FREE MEN'S MINDS!

Another version flashed by his car:

> DISBAND THE TERRORIST THOUGHT-
> CONTROL SECRET POLICE
> END CONCENTRATION SLAVE LABOR
> CAMPS
> RESTORE FREEDOM AND LIBERTY!

Simpler slogans . . . and the most effective:

> ON TO THE STARS

The illuminated banners flashed everywhere; he couldn't help being thrilled. There was a wild excitement about it, a furious festive sense of meaning in the idea of breaking out of the system, reaching the stars, the other systems, the endless other suns. He wasn't exempt; he wanted it, too.

Utopia. The Golden Age. They had not found it on Earth; the last war had made them see it was never coming. From Earth they had turned to the other planets; they had built up romantic fiction, told themselves pleasant lies. The other planets, they said, were green, fertile worlds, water-sparkling valleys, thick-wooded hills. Paradise: the ancient, eternal hope. But the other planets were nightmares of frozen methane gas, miles of stark rock. Without life or sound, only the blowing death of rocks and gas and empty darkness.

But the followers of Jones had not given up; they had a dream, a vision. They were sure the Second Earth existed. Somehow, somebody had contrived to keep it from them: there was a conspiracy going on. It was Fedgov on Earth; Relativism was stifling them. Beyond Earth, it was the drifters. Once Fedgov was gone, once the drifters had been destroyed . . . the old story. Green pastures, beyond the very next hill.

Yet, it was not disgust that Cussick felt for the dreaming, racing figures. It was admiration. They were idealists. He, on the other hand, was only a realist. And he was ashamed.

On every street corner loomed a brightly-lit table with projecting sign. At each table an organization worker sat with a petition, collecting names from the lines of waiting people.

UNIVERSAL REFERENDUM. DEMAND
FEDGOV STEP ASIDE AND APPOINT
JONES SUPREME COMMANDER TO DEAL
WITH THE PRESENT CRISIS

That was the chilling sight: the lines of tired people, worn out from a long hard day of work, willing to stand patiently in line. Not the enthusiastic faces of the dedicated followers, but these drab, ordinary citizens desiring to abolish their legal government, wishing to end a government of law and to create in its place an authority of absolute will: the unqualified whim of an individual person.

As he climbed the steps to his apartment, Cussick made out a faint high-pitched squeal. His mind, leaden and sunk in despondency, failed to react; it wasn't until he had the front door unlocked and was turning on the light that he identified the alarm signal of the vidphone.

When he snapped the set on, a visual tape-image appeared with a brief recorded message. Director Pearson's face, stern and harsh, rose up and confronted him. "I want you back at the office," Pearson stated. "Get over here immediately; this cancels everything else." The image clicked, then resumed. Once more Pearson's withered mouth opened and words came out. "I want you back at the office. Get over here immediately; this cancels everything else." It was beginning a third time when Cussick cut it savagely off and allowed the set to die.

At first he was blindly annoyed. He was tired; he wanted to eat dinner and go to bed. And there was the possibility, discussed in general, abstract terms, of taking Tyler out to a show. For an instant he considered ignoring the message; Pearson had no way to check up—he might not get home for hours.

Thinking about it, Cussick stepped into the empty, deserted kitchen and began fixing himself a sandwich. By the time he had finished he had made up his mind. Hurrying back out of the apartment, he strode down the stairs to the garage and rapidly backed out his car. Eating his sandwich on the way, he drove at high speed back to the police buildings. Something Tyler had said, something that seemed unimportant at the time, all at once made terrifying sense.

Pearson admitted him immediately. "Here's the situation," he explained. "Your pal Kaminski, at three-thirty this afternoon, packed up his reports, stuffed as much classified material into his briefcase as he could, and skipped."

Paralyzed, Cussick could say nothing. Foolishly, he stood wiping sandwich crumbs from his mouth.

"We weren't surprised," Pearson continued, reading from a memo, standing with his feet apart behind his desk, a grim, upright figure of a man. "We caught him a hundred miles up and forced his ship down."

"Where was he going?" Cussick managed. But he already knew.

"He had a little deal cooked up with the Jones people. Something he's been fretting about for months. In return for his data they were going to provide him with sanctuary. They had some sort of retreat fixed up; Kaminski was going to hide away and sit out the war or whatever's coming. He washed his hands of it; he was through. And, of course, he couldn't resign. Nobody resigns from the police, these days. Not in this emergency."

"What did you do with him? Where is he?"

"He's in the Saskatchewan labor camp. For the rest of his life. He's already been taken there; I had them take him right off. I'm making this public; I want this to be an example."

"But," Cussick said hoarsely, "he's sick. He's old and ill. He doesn't know what he's doing. He's gone all to pieces—he ought to be in a hospital, not a forced labor camp!"

"He ought to be shot. Only we don't shoot people anymore. All we can do is put them to work for the rest of their lives. Your old instructor will be sorting bolts until he's dead." Pearson came out from behind his desk. "I'm telling you this because you're partly responsible. We've been keeping an eye on all of you; Kaminski and that ex-Communist girl, Tyler Fleming, and your wife. We know your wife is a Jones agent; we know she's been working with them, living at one of their meeting units, getting indoctrination—giving them money." Folding up his memo, he added, "Kaminski knew about it. He held up the information—tried to suppress it."

"He didn't want me to know," Cussick said.

"He didn't want *us* to know, you mean. We realized the chances were high that he'd take off, after your wife left you and crossed over completely. We expected him to follow, sooner or later. As far as you're concerned—" Pearson shrugged. "I don't think there's a chance in the world you'd do what he'd done. That girl, too; she's still with us. But it's a nasty business." Suddenly the harshness left his voice. "It's a terrible thing . . . that wonderful old man. I thought you ought to know."

"Thanks," Cussick said numbly.

"Probably you're right. Certainly he ought to be in a hospital. But we can't do that; we're fighting for our lives. A lot of us want to get out . . . maybe all of us."

"Maybe so," Cussick agreed, barely hearing him.

"The Jones people are getting in everywhere. The whole structure is crumbling; every class, every group. Here in Security, men are slipping off, vanishing . . . like Kaminski. I had to put him in a work camp. If I could, I'd kill him in cold blood."

"But you wouldn't want to."

"No," Pearson agreed. "I wouldn't want to. But I'd do it." For a moment he was silent. Then he went on: "Kaminski was handling the security program for a top-secret Fedgov project. Something under the Department of Health . . . I don't know what it is; nobody does, here. The Council knows, of course. It's the work of a biochemist named Rafferty. You've probably heard of him; he disappeared about thirty years ago."

"I remember," Cussick said vaguely; he couldn't bring his mind into focus. "Is Max all right? He's not injured, is he?"

"He's all right." Impatiently, Pearson want on: "You'll have to take over the security aspect of this project. I suppose that son of a bitch Jones knows all about it; we stopped Kaminski from taking his papers, but Jones may have got an oral report." Furiously, he snapped: "Anyhow, Jones can't do anything. He's not in power—yet. And until he is, we're protecting this project."

Stupidly, Cussick asked: "What do you want me to do?"

"Obviously, I'm sending you over to Rafferty so you can find out what it's all about." From his desk Pearson snatched a packet of identification papers and held them out. "Rafferty had already been notified about Kaminski. He's expecting you; everything has been set up. Get right over there and report to me as soon as you think you've got it untangled. Not the project—I don't want to hear about that. All I'm interested in is the security end. Understand?"

In a daze, Cussick made his way out of the office. A high-velocity police cruiser was idling at the curb; three weapons-cops stood around in their shiny helmets, gripping regulation machine guns. They came instantly to attention as he stumbled up to them, shocked and confused, hardly able to grasp what was happening.

"I don't know anything about this," he informed them. "I don't know where we're going."

"We already have our orders, sir," one of the weapons-cops told him. "We've got the route plotted."

A moment later he was rising up above the dark city, with no idea of his destination. To his right, one of the cops had fallen into a contented half-sleep, his gun resting in his lap. The ship was on robot pilot; the other two cops were beginning to play cards. Cussick settled back and prepared for a long trip.

The trip, however, ended abruptly. All at once the ship nosed down; one of the cops laid aside his hand of cards and resumed manual control. Below, in the darkness, stretched the winking lights of a great city. It wasn't until the ship had actually come to rest on a roof-top field that Cussick recognized it, San Francisco. Then this was what Kaminski had meant, that night. *Near them* . . . the project he had mumbled about, brooded over, but not discussed. Now he would learn what it was all about—but he wasn't thinking about the Fedgov project. He was thinking about Kaminski in the forced labor camp.

With a click the hull slid aside and the three cops filed out. Cautiously, Cussick made his way down. Incredibly chill wind whipped around him; shivering, he peered to see where he was. In the downtown business section, apparently. The grand opaque shapes of office buildings loomed up in the frigid gloom.

"What now?" he inquired irritably.

He was led along a ramp, through an intricate multiseal lock and down a flight of metal steps. A moment later he was facing a small, rather modest-appearing elderly man in a white medical uniform. The gentleman removed his glasses, blinked, and held out his hand. Rafferty was unassuming, with a worried, preoccupied twitch to his dry features. Above his lips was the faint wisp of an unsuccessful mustache.

"Yes," he acknowledged, as they shook hands, "I'm Rafferty. But they're not here, now. You'll have to wait."

Cussick said: "Doctor, I don't know anything about this." He got out the papers Pearson had given him and handed them over. "I was called into this without warning. You got word about Kaminski?"

Rafferty glanced suspiciously around, then turned and started off down the corridor. As Cussick walked beside him, the biochemist explained: "I sent them off when Pearson notified me that Kaminski had crossed over. It was my idea; I wanted them out of here, in case Kaminski had carried information to the Jones people. Sort of a silly gesture; if Jones knows now, he knew one year ago. But I thought there might be an attack . . . I've watched those mobs climb up on buildings after those protoplasmic affairs. I thought they might come here—using that as a pretext."

"Where are you taking me?" Cussick asked.

"I'm going to show you the project. I have to, if you're handling security. My God, you can't take care of them if you don't understand what they are."

Cussick found himself in an elaborate maze of white-glistening, hygienic passages. Doctors wandered here and there, involved in medical work beyond his comprehension. None of them paid any attention to him.

"This is their Refuge," Rafferty explained, as he stopped before an elongated transparent wall. "I'm having the whole shell cleaned and serviced while they're out of it. Killing two birds with one stone." He examined a series of wall-gauges. "We'll be able to go inside, in a few minutes."

Cussick was looking into an enormous steamy tank. Clouds of dense moisture billowed, obscuring the macabre land-scape. Machinery was at work, lumbering through the humid atmosphere, spraying from thin nozzles. The ground was spongy in appearance. Occasional thick shrubs had sprouted; lumps of vegetable matter completely alien to him. Pools of humid water oozed over the ground. Only greens and blues were visible; the whole tank resembled a marine world, rather than a land world.

"The atmosphere," Rafferty explained, "is a compound of ammonia, oxygen, freon, and traces of methane. You can see how wet it is. The temperature is high, for us—usually around a hundred degrees Fahrenheit."

Cussick could make out the sight of buildings half-lost in the dense clouds of water vapor. Small structures, their sides glistening, dripping fat drops of moisture. A damp world, hot, steamy, compact. And utterly unfamiliar.

"They live in there?" he asked slowly.

"The Refuge is their medium. It was constructed to meet

their needs, a closed enclave designed to keep them alive. They call it their womb; actually, it's more an incubator: a transitionary membrane between the womb and the world. But they're never coming out to this world."

A technician approached; he and Rafferty conferred.

"All right," Rafferty said. "We can go inside, now."

A series of wall locks slid aside, and the two men entered the Refuge. Cussick choked, as burning swirls of gas blew up around him. He halted, stumbled, got out his handkerchief and clapped it over his nose.

"You'll get used to it," Rafferty said wryly.

"It's like going into a steam bath. Worse." Cussick was violently perspiring; he couldn't breathe and he couldn't see. As they walked along, Rafferty calmly explained the situation.

"They can't live outside of this, and we can't live in here. So this Refuge has to be carefully maintained. It's possible to destroy them simply by opening a few valves, by letting out their air and letting ours in. Or by smashing the wall. Or by allowing it to cool off. Or by cutting their food supply; obviously, their systems require a totally different diet from our own. Kaminski always did an excellent job of protecting the Refuge; he's had secret-service men scattered around everywhere. Nobody, not even I, can get into this building without being checked by one of your men."

As the lumbering machines worked, the air gradually cleared. Now Cussick could see a trifle. And the thick wad of gas jammed into his lungs was beginning to dissolve. "Where did you send them?"

"There's a very small alternate area. So we can get in here periodically and go over it in detail." Rafferty indicated the work-teams making their way into the Refuge; the whole upper surface had been removed to make way for major equipment. "Not a duplicate of this: only a portable van.

And it gives them a sense of getting out. We'll pick them up around two o'clock; they like to stay as long as possible. I'll take you inside their living quarters."

Cussick had to stoop over to get through the door. "They must be short," he commented.

"Very short, very small. Luis, the heaviest, weighs less than a hundred pounds." Rafferty halted. "This is their kitchen. Chairs, table. Dishes."

Everything was in miniature. A doll's house: tiny furniture, tiny silverware, a replica of any kitchen but on a reduced scale. From the table, Cussick picked up a wax-impregnated copy of the *Wall Street Journal*. "They read this?" he demanded, incredulous.

"Certainly." Rafferty took him down a tiny corridor and into a side room. "This is the quarters of one of them—Frank, his name is. Look around. You'll see books, recording tapes, clothing like our own. These are people! Human beings, in the cultural, spiritual, moral, and psychological sense. Intellectually, they're as close to us as—" He gestured. "Closer to us than some of those howling maniacs out there, with their signs and slogans."

"My God," Cussick said, locating a chess set, an electric razor, a pair of suspenders and, tacked up on the wall, a girlie calendar. On the dresser was a book edition of James Joyce's *Ulysses*. "They're mutants, aren't they? Wartime deviants?"

"No," Rafferty answered, "they're my children."

"Figuratively, you mean."

"No, I mean literally. I'm their father. Their embryos were removed from my wife's womb and placed in an artificial membrane. I sired each one of them; my wife and I are the parents of the whole group."

"But," Cussick said slowly, "then they're deliberate mutants."

"Certainly. For over thirty years I've worked with them, developing them according to our program. Each one is a little more perfected. We've learned a lot . . . most of the first ones died."

"How many are there?"

"There have been forty, in all. But only eight are alive: seven in the Refuge and one infant still in a separate incubator. It's delicate work, and we have no body of knowledge to draw from." The drab little doctor spoke calmly; he was merely stating facts. His kind of pride went beyond any boasting.

"Artificially-bred mutants," Cussick said, prowling around the cramped room. "That's why they have a common environment."

"You've seen some of the war-time sports?"

"Quite a few."

"Then you won't be shocked. It's a little difficult to take, at first. And in a way, I suppose, it's almost funny. I've seen doctors laugh out loud. They're small; they're frail; they have a kind of worried frown. Like me. They toil around the Refuge; they argue and discourse and fight and fret and make love. They have a complete community. The Refuge is their world and in it they form a total organic society."

"What's their purpose?" Cussick demanded. Dimly, he was already beginning to grasp the point of the project. "If they can't live outside, on Earth—"

"That's it," Rafferty said, matter-of-factly. "They're not supposed to live on Earth. They're intended to live on Venus. We tried to develop a group for survival on Mars, but nothing came of it. Mars and Earth are too different—but Venus is a little more likely. This Refuge, this miniature world, is an exact replica of the conditions our scout ships found on Venus."

12

Outside the miniature compound building, Doctor Rafferty bent down and showed Cussick one of the sponges indigenous to the Refuge. "This is artificial. But there are legitimate sponges like this on Venus; they were brought here and our teams made models."

"Why not simply transplant them? Won't the real thing grow in here?"

"I'll explain why, a little later." Getting to his feet he led Cussick to the edge of a small lapping lake. "And these are fakes, too." From the water Rafferty grabbed a wriggling snake-like creature, with short, stubby legs that thrashed furiously. Swiftly, Rafferty twisted the head; the head came off and the creature stopped moving. "A mechanical contraption—you can see the wiring. But again, an exact model of genuine Venusian fauna." He restored the head; once more the creature began flopping. Rafferty tossed it back in the water and it swam happily off.

"Those mountains," Cussick said, pointing up. "That's a backdrop based on the Venusian scene?"

"Right." Rafferty started briskly off. "We can go up there, if you want. They step around their mountains all the time."

As the two men strode from rock to rock, Rafferty went on with his explanation.

"This Refuge is a school, as well as an environment. It's designed to shape them, to equate them to a nonterrestrial milieu. When they go to Venus, they'll be prepared—at least, as well as we can arrange. Probably some of them will die; they may very well be damaged by the change. After all, we can't be infallible; we've done the best we can to imitate conditions there, but it's not letter-perfect."

"Wait," Cussick interrupted. "They themselves—they're not modeled after Venusian humanoid life-forms?"

"No," Rafferty agreed. "They're new creations, not imitations. The original human embryos were altered on the phenotype principle: we subjected them to nonterrestrial conditions—specifically, to a scale of stresses similar to those operating on Venus. The stresses were intricate; we had plenty of failures. As soon as the altered babies were born they were popped into V-type incubators: media again reproducing the Venusian pattern. In other words, we warped each embryo, and we continued to apply the stresses after the babies were born. As you realize, if human colonists land on Venus they won't survive. Fedgov has tried that; it's a matter of record. But if there were a few specific physical changes, it might be possible to keep a colony alive. If we could arrange graded steps, in-between stages, locks through which they could pass . . . *acclimatization* is what we wanted. Adaptation, actually. In time, we knew, the progeny would mutate in response to external pressures. Gradually, subsequent generations would be remolded along survival lines. Many would die but some would struggle along. Eventually we'd have a quasi-human species, not physically like ourselves, but, nonetheless, human beings. Altered men, fit to live on Venus."

"I see," Cussick said. "This is Fedgov's solution."

"Absolutely. We'll never find the exact conditions we have

here on Earth—no two planets are identical. Good God, we're lucky to find Venus, a planet with our density, with gravity, moisture, warmth. Naturally, it's a literal hell for you and me. But it doesn't take much to turn heaven into hell— a rise in temperature of ten degrees, an increase of one percent humidity." Kicking at a blue-black lichen creeping up the side of a flat rock, Rafferty continued: "We could have waited a thousand years, done it the long way. Fed human settlers in, one load after another, sent off countless ships, started a colony. People would have died like flies. They would have been miserable. Nature can afford it, but we can't. Our people would have loathed it."

"Yes," Cussick agreed, "that's already been shown."

"Eventually, the results would have been the same. But would we have been willing to take the losses? I think we would have backed down. We don't have thousands of years and millions of lives to give; we would have given up, pulled our colonies home. Because, in the final analysis, we don't want to adapt to other planets: we want them to conform to us. Even if we found one second Earth it wouldn't be enough. Here, in this project, we have the seed of a much greater future. If this works, if the Venus mutants survive, we can go on and perfect our techniques. Develop mutant colonies for various other planets, for more radical environments. Eventually, we can populate the universe—survive anywhere. If we succeed, we'll have conquered totally. The human species will be indestructible. This Refuge, this closed enclave, and my work—all this looks artificial. But what I've done is try to speed up natural evolution. I've tried to systemize it, cut out the randomness, the waste, the aimlessness of it. Instead of sending Earthmen to Venus we're going to send *Venusians*. When they get there, they won't find an alien, hostile world; they'll find their *real* world, the genuine world they've already known—as a model. They'll find the ultimate realization of this cramped replica."

"Do they know this?"

"No."

"Why not?"

"Because," Rafferty said, "it was essential they think nobody was responsible for their situation. If they had known we deliberately altered them, made them unfit to live on Earth, they would never have forgiven us. Over two decades in this Refuge—victims of a scientific experiment. They've always been told they're natural mutants, war-time mutants, like the others. They were picked without their permission. They were involuntary subjects, and many of them died. You think they would ever have forgiven us, knowing we had done this to them?"

"But they'll find out eventually."

"They'll find out when they reach Venus. Then, for all practical purposes, it doesn't matter. Because we won't be there; they'll be on their own. Resentment will be absurd at that point. They'll be glad of their alteration—good God, it'll mean survival! On Venus you and I would be the freaks, incapable of survival. On Venus *we* would need Refuges."

After a thoughtful moment, Cussick asked: "When can I see these Venusians?"

"I'll arrange it. Within a few days, certainly. All this turmoil has upset our routine, and they feel it, too. They're as tense as we are."

Twenty-four hours later, while he was involved in transferring his papers to San Francisco, Cussick saw the Venusian mutants for the first time.

At the bottom floor of the building Doctor Rafferty met him. It was two o'clock in the morning and the street was cold and foggy. "I called you because this is an excellent opportunity," Rafferty said, guiding him toward the ascent ramp. "Our small friends get somewhat excited, once in awhile. They've decided they can lick any man in the house."

• • •

After the Van had returned the half-conscious mutants to their Refuge, Cussick and Rafferty stood together on the fog-drenched sidewalk. The futility of the mutants' struggle hung in the darkness; both men felt the oppressive nearness of defeat.

"Maybe you're right about Jones," Rafferty said finally. "Maybe he's only human." He got out his car keys and started toward his parked car. "But it's like fighting the ocean. We're going under, sinking every day. A civilization drowning in the deluge. The new flood."

"The divine force," Cussick said ironically.

"We can't destroy Jones. We can only hope there's something beyond him, something on the other side." Rafferty opened his car door and got in. "You can dismantle the street-blocks if you want. But keep them handy."

"I will," Cussick said. "Good night."

"Good night," Rafferty said. The motor started, and the car drove off. Cussick was left alone. Chill tendrils of fog billowed around him: he shivered, realizing how it must have seemed to the four mutants. Frail little creatures with their hopes, their confused dreams, not knowing who or what they were . . . and outside their glass womb, waiting for them, the night and the gray marching shapes: the Jones Organization.

Cussick walked slowly along the dark sidewalk until he came to the first police barricade. "Okay," he told the helmeted sergeant. "You can unscramble it now."

The sergeant paid no attention to him; the squad of police were standing around their relay phones, listening fixedly to a closed-circuit audiocast.

Irritably, Cussick started to grab the officer by the shoulder. About that time he comprehended what he was hearing; he forgot the sergeant, Rafferty, the barricades, the Venusian mutants. Crouching down, he forced his way close to the speaker; rigidly, he listened.

". . . the first stages of the attack brought into Security hands at least fifty percent of the criminal ringleaders. Throughout major metropolitan areas, weapons-teams are rounding up remaining policy-level personnel. The action is proceeding in orderly fashion . . . there is very little overt resistance. Reverend Floyd Jones himself has been reported wounded in a skirmish between his supporters and police units. A report from New York describes major street fighting between fanatical mobs and police tanks. All weapons-police in that area are ordered to report to their dispatch points; previous instructions are automatically cancelled. To repeat the original notification: the Supreme Council of the Federal World Government has declared the organization designated as Patriots United to be illegal, and all members of said organization are hereby classed as criminal elements. The enabling legislation instructs secret-service police to arrest on sight and turn over to Public Courts all members of the organization Patriots United, and all persons affiliated with subgroups such as the Youth Loyalty League, the Women's . . ."

Cussick turned away, his body half-frozen with the night cold. He stamped his feet, blew on his hands, flapped his arms around him. So Pearson had gone into action. The Council had ratified his program: Jones and his organization were being rounded up, sentenced, and dispersed to various labor camps. Under Clause Two, probably, the statute giving Security the authority to arrest members of charismatic cults that threatened the free dissemination of the principles of Relativism. A deliberately vague clause, put on the books as catch-all legislation: to cover any and all situations not otherwise controlled.

But Jones must have known. The organization must have

expected the attack. One year ago, Jones must have anticipated that in his stern outrage, Pearson would go ahead, would make one great final effort to smash the burgeoning movement. Kaminski's betrayal had goaded Pearson on; he wanted to move, do something, make some last attempt to save Fedgov, before the whole thing was decided. But in Jones' mind it had already been decided.

As he stood listening to the police audiocast, Cussick wondered how Jones could possibly be caught off guard. Arrested and wounded. Unless, of course, he wanted to be arrested. Unless it was his plan to be shot. In that case, Pearson had probably sealed the final disposition of Fedgov.

Possibly, even probably, Pearson, in his furious desire to act, had made Jones' victory an absolute certainty.

13

The crowd roared. In the afternoon of that historic day the crowd blurred in the heat of the sun, and its combined voices thundered approval of the small man standing on the platform, the tiny figure that gestured and spoke and waved its arms. Loudspeakers carried the speech, amplified the original voice until it bellowed over the surge of crowd-noise. Beyond the mass of people were the ruins that had been Frankfurt, Germany.

"My friends," Jones shouted, "the entrenched plutocracy has tried to silence me. But they have grown soft; like great parasites they sit behind their desks running the world. They have grown fat on us; they have feasted well. But it is going to end. I can see it."

Shouted approval.

"We must strike out!" Jones raved on. "Beyond the world, beyond the dead systems. It is our destiny. The race cannot be denied its future. Nothing will stop us. We cannot be defeated."

On and on he went. And somewhere, standing silently among the spectators, untouched by the feverish harangue, waited the police assassin.

He had been a soldier in the war. He was a crack shot, with a suitcase full of medals. In the last stages of the war he became a professional assassin. The chance of his shot missing the target was one in a million.

On the day of the speech, Pratt was driven from the labor camp at Manresa, Spain, to the outskirts of Frankfurt. As the long, lowslung car purred over the twisting roads, he went over in his mind the way he was going to do it. There wasn't much to think about; his whole body was geared to the job ahead. After awhile he put his head back against the luxurious seat and enjoyed the pull of the powerful turbine.

The car let him off in a deserted area, a patch of ruin and gaping bomb craters that hadn't been reconstructed. Pratt sat down among the ruins, got out his lunch, and ate. Then he wiped his mouth, picked up his rifle, and trudged toward town. It was one-thirty; he had plenty of time. Along the road moved people and vehicles, a constant swell of individuals moving in to hear Jones. Pratt joined them; he was one of many. As he walked, he carried his rifle openly. It was a war-rifle, the one he had used in the final confused days. His decorations permitted him to carry it; the rifle was a badge of honor.

The speech did not interest him. He was too practical a man to be moved by the excited tumult of words. As Jones shouted and gestured, the lean-jawed soldier prowled around, looking for the point at which the march would originate, the spot where Jones would take command of his gray troopers.

This part of Frankfurt still lay in rubble. A residential section, it was the last to be repaired. The inhabitants were living in temporary barracks erected by the Government. As Jones' speech came to an end, groups of organization workers collected here and there, obviously in pre-arranged patterns. Pratt, standing with his rifle, watched with interest.

Before him lay what looked like a cement wheel. The wheel

was a solid mass of followers, assembled together in a single grim heap. The crossed-retort flag fluttered on all sides. Everybody had armbands or uniforms. Ahead of the wheel of gray lay an open stretch of Landstrasse, the still undamaged highway leading into the town. The highway had existed from the time of the Third Reich; it had been constructed by the Nazi engineering genius, Doktor Todt, and his O. T. Gruppe. It was an excellent highway. In a little while, the gray wheel would unwind and march down it, toward the town.

The police had carefully cleared all traffic from the highway. Police patrols walked up and down the deserted strip, waving people angrily back. A few children and a stray dog scampered excitedly ahead of them.

The noise was already deafening. Milling lumps of spectators were breaking away from the nearby field, making toward the assembly point. Pratt winced as groups surged against him, their eyes glassy, mouths open and half-clogged with stale cheers. Lifting his rifle he climbed up on a heap of rubble, out of the way.

A corps of newspaper reporters with flash cameras were taking pictures of the crowd and the gray mass of organization agents that formed the first ranks. Helmeted police were everywhere, in pairs and threes. They all carried weapons; they looked cruel and uneasy in their brown uniforms. Where the stretch of highway began, four ambulances had been parked, two on each side. Elaborate TV equipment had been set up nearby; the technicians and medical teams stood joking and lounging. The reporters took pictures of them, too. They were taking pictures of everything.

Pratt made his way with caution. He managed to slide through the final fringes of the crowd and out into the open. A moment later he was standing at the main police barricade, erected at the edge of the highway. The uniformed cops gazed at him blankly; he wasn't known to them. One of them, a giant with a vast moon-like face, detached himself and came striding ominously over, his machine gun raised.

"Get over to the other side!" he yelled at Pratt. "Get off the highway!"

The police were stretching heavy white rope on both sides of the pavement, to keep the march confined. They wanted to be sure it went in the right direction; it was supposed to go where the weapons-units waited.

"God damn you!" the big cop yelled. "I told you to get out of here! You want to get killed?"

"Where's McHaffie?" Pratt said.

"Who are you?"

Pratt located Police Major McHaffie, the officer in charge of the detail. Approaching him, he showed his identification. "All right," McHaffie muttered, preoccupied. He didn't know what Pratt's mission was, only that he was on a Security job. "Get up there on one of the trucks; that's where you'll get the best view. The stupid bastards are starting any minute."

McHaffie had picked a good place for the barricade. Once the marchers had gone past it toward the city, the trucks would cut through the rope and swing around, blocking the highway. Then, as the crowd streamed back, the police teams would sort through them. Caught between two police walls, Jones and his followers would be trapped like cattle. More trucks were waiting: to take the followers off to forced labor camps.

The barricade itself was formidable. He doubted if the mob—and it would be a mob by that time—could break it. Trucks, plus heavy guns, and maybe a line of tanks. He wasn't too familiar with that part. This would be the initial police attack: Jones dead, the policy-level followers rounded up. And then, all over the world, city by city, the rest would be netted. Over a period of days, perhaps weeks, the roundup would continue. Slowly, efficiently.

Reaching up to the truck, Pratt began to climb. Six or seven hands reached to help him; he sprawled awkwardly, clutching his rifle and struggling, until somebody helped him to his feet. He brushed himself off and found a place near the front. He wasn't the only one with a war-rifle; several flashed in the afternoon sunlight. As he stood his gun upright, nobody paid attention. They were all watching the marchers.

"This is a good location," he said to McHaffie, as the police major followed after him.

McHaffie eyed the rifle. "What's that you have there? An old A-5? I wish you guys had thrown them away." Obviously, he thought Pratt was a bellicose war veteran, nothing more. "We ought to have yanked the firing pins out."

"There're a lot of people down there," a sergeant observed uneasily.

"You think they'll get by us?" another asked nervously, a young kid. "They're crazy—they might do anything."

"I don't think so," McHaffie said vaguely, peering at the mob through his binoculars.

"They want to get killed," the sergeant said. "That's what they're out there for. They can see us—Jones must know we're going to close in on them. Can't he see the future? Isn't that his line?"

Warm wind smacked at them from the ruins and half-filled craters. In the distance, across the hazy sky, a row of transports moved slowly, inexorably. The men in the trucks were restless and irritable; they whacked their guns against the metal hull around them, spat over the edge, shaded their eyes against the bright sun and peered angrily at the gray wheel of marchers.

"It won't be long," McHaffie commented. The crowd was obediently forming behind the gray phalanx.

"How many do you figure are there?" Pratt asked.

"Thousands. Millions. I guess the big cheese is going to ride in his car while the others walk." McHaffie indicated a parked limousine. "One of his rich backers gave that to him."

"He's supposed to be out front," a reporter said, over-hearing McHaffie. "According to the crap they put out, he'll be right up there marching at the head."

"I think he will," Pratt said.

"You know anything about him?" the reporter demanded, his puffy face slack and avid at once. He was a typical Berlin newspaper man, in baggy tweeds, a pipe in his mouth, cynical and aloof.

"No," Pratt said.

"Is it true Jones is an escaped con from the Bolivian forced labor camps?"

"I heard he used to be with a freak show," the sergeant said. "He's a mutant, one of those war-time sports."

Pratt said nothing. His head ached from the glare and the dust blown by the dry wind. He wished things would hurry.

"Look," the reporter said to McHaffie. "Let me ask you something. Those guys there. What is it, some sort of racket? What's the story on this thing?"

"Get going," McHaffie muttered.

"Isn't it a racket? What's Jones in it for? He's got a lot of rich backers—right? He's a minister or something. This is a cult—right? Rich people kick in money and a lot of swank clothes and cars and jewelry, he has all the babes he wants—right?"

Nobody answered.

Presently the reporter addressed himself to a tall thin cop, who stood pressed against the railing, his arms full of rocket-firing equipment. "Hey," the reporter said softly. "Is this really a Fedgov stunt? To whip up interest in colonization? They going to spring a big immigration deal? Let me in on it."

"Christ," the reporter muttered plaintively, "I'm just trying to understand this thing. There must be an angle . . . I'm trying to figure out what he's in it for."

A short, red-faced cop swarmed up onto the truck, carrying telephone lines. "I'm glad I'm up here," he panted to McHaffie. "That's going to be a mess when they hit the blocks in town."

The reporter put his hand on the man's shoulder. "Hey, friend," he said, "what the hell is all this? What are those loons in this for?"

Catching his breath, the red-faced cop paused. "It's not a racket."

"Then what are they after? Give me the word."

"If it was a racket we wouldn't have any trouble. We could buy them off."

"That's interesting." The reporter eyed him languidly. "You ever met this Jones?"

"No," the red-faced cop admitted. "But my wife shook hands with him once." He added: "She's a member."

The reporter was incredulous. "No kidding?"

"She's probably down there marching."

"Take off," McHaffie snapped at the red-faced policeman. "Report back to your unit."

The cop obediently pushed to the back of the truck and leaped down onto the highway.

The reporter scratched a few notes on a pad of paper and then put it away. He eyed Pratt's rifle curiously. "What's that you got there, Dad?" he asked.

Pratt said nothing. He was feeling worse each minute, as the sun glared above them. His mouth was dry and acid. The touch of an ancient malaria shivered through him, bringing its weakness and chills. It was always this way, before a kill.

"That's a wicked-looking hunk of metal," the reporter observed. "You going to blow some guy's head off with that?"

"Get out of here, you big-mouth bastard," the thin cop grated, "before he blows your ass off with it."

"Jesus," the reporter said. "You guys are sure touchy."

He edged toward the far side of the truck. "You're as bad as those loons down there."

Pratt wiped sweat from his upper lip and steadied the rifle against the side of the truck. The metal shone bright and hot in the furious heat. His eyes burned, and his legs were beginning to wobble. He wondered how long it would be before the gray started unwinding and flowing forward. Not long, probably.

"Let me use your glasses," he said to McHaffie.

"Don't drop them." McHaffie passed the binoculars over; his hands were shaking. "Christ, this thing is getting me. If anything goes wrong, I'll be in a labor camp along with them."

Pratt gazed through the binoculars at the wheel of gray, with its dense and obedient mob packed in behind it. Jones had arrived. He was standing in front, conversing with the organization workers. Now the marchers were being formed in columns of ten; a long snake with its gray head on the edge of the highway and its body out among the ruins. The waiting marchers milled and pushed. Pratt could hear them, a thin constant din. They were shouting and yelling as loud as they could.

"Hear them?" he said to McHaffie.

"Give me back my glasses; I think they're starting."

"They're not starting." Pratt adjusted the focus-screw. There was his prey: the small, gaunt, familiar man, with his steel-rimmed glasses, unimpressive, unimportant-looking. That was Jones.

"Come on!" McHaffie shrieked. "Let's have them!"

Pratt returned the binoculars. McHaffie quickly swept them up and refocussed them. "By God," he whispered, "here they come. They've started."

The columns of gray had moved onto the highway. The yelling, shouting crowd was creeping along behind them. Dogs barked furiously. Children ran back and forth in frenzied excitement. On the trucks, the weapons-police shuffled uneasily and raised their guns.

Jones, at the head of the columns, marched with jerky, uneven strides, directly down the center of the highway. A quick, mechanical pace, like a wound-up doll. Without the binoculars, Pratt could not make out his face; Jones was still a long way off. He grabbed up his rifle and threw off the safety catch. Raising it, he stood tense and expectant. Around him, those with guns were doing the same.

"Remember," McHaffie muttered, "don't fire. Let them past; let them beyond the barricade. Then get ready to close in."

On one of the trucks a policeman teetered, then fell sprawling onto the highway. He rolled, quickly picked himself up, and scampered in panic for safety beyond the white rope.

"Bring up the first trucks," McHaffie ordered into his phone.

The columns of marchers were moving past the barricade. Some of them glanced fearfully at the parked trucks, the crouching police.

"Get them up!" McHaffie screamed. "Start the motors, you jackasses!"

The first of the marchers had passed the barricade. Coming from Frankfurt was the first line of police tanks; the other jaw of the trap was closing. The marchers would never reach town. With shrieking roars, truck motors came to life. Driving around behind the marchers, the trucks flowed out onto the highway, cutting them off. Abruptly, the marchers halted. Roars of dismay rose above the thunder of motors. The columns broke and wavered; the long gray snake suddenly dissected itself. Those behind hesitated. Those ahead began to mill in confusion.

"They're in," McHaffie was tonelessly saying. "They're between."

The marchers were not moving forward. Jones had halted;

he stood peering warily around. Like a little rat, Pratt thought. A dirty little yellow-toothed rat. He raised his rifle and aimed.

Now the whole crowd was in motion. The mass that had been heading up the highway split into aimless pieces, people hurrying in various directions, off the highway, through the rope; it made no difference. Fast-moving police cars were racing along the rim of the ruins, herding them back. It was chaos. Pratt paid no attention; he saw only the small, thin figure of Jones.

"You're under arrest!" loudspeakers boomed. "Stop moving and stand still. You're under Security arrest!"

Some of the people halted. Stricken faces turned upward; air-borne police units were landing. A group of organization toughs broke into life and raced toward a police team. Clubs swinging, the toughs crashed head-on into the waiting unit; a tangled mass of gray and brown struggled on the pavement. More marchers fled from the highway toward the ruins beyond. On foot, running police batted them down; clouds of thick dust rose, obscuring the scene. The air was filled with screams and crashing roars. A truck groaned, then slid gradually on its side. A wall of crazed fanatics had pushed it over.

Aiming carefully, Pratt fired.

His bullet missed Jones entirely. Stunned, he threw the bolt and again raised the rifle. As he had fired, Jones miraculously, inexplicably, had stepped aside. A split second— it was incredible. Obviously, Jones had expected it.

Scrambling from his truck onto the next, Pratt made his way around the edge of the crowd. He leaped down onto a mass of ruins; grasping his rifle, he gained a precarious footing and loped rapidly forward. This time he would fire from a few feet away; this time he would be directly in front of Jones.

Dropping to the highway, Pratt forced his way into the crowd. Using the butt of his rifle as a club, he beat his way among them. A bottle burst over his head; for an interval darkness swirled, and he floundered against a mass of wildly struggling human bodies. Then he dragged himself up and crept on.

All at once, he was sprawling. Clutching the rifle, he rolled to his feet and managed to get to his knees before a gray-clad shape smashed him with a length of pipe. This time he lost teeth; warm blood gushed down his throat, choking him. Blinded, he lay gasping. Huge, crushing boots stamped on his ribs; he shrieked, groped upward, caught hold of a trouser leg, and tugged. The figure stumbled and fell. Pratt rolled on him, his hands around a section of broken bottle. With a swift stroke he cut the man's throat, pushed the body away, and climbed up.

Ahead of him was a cleared spot, a dead center in the maelstrom of frenzied shapes. Jones stood inert; behind his glasses, his eyes darted frantically. Around him had grouped a knot of organization fighters, a last-ditch defense.

Kneeling, Pratt managed to get his rifle up. Flickering mists danced in front of him; he was suspended in a silent, unmoving interval. Automatically, his fingers squeezed the trigger; there was no noise, only a faint shudder of the gun stock.

He saw Jones stumble, clutch at his belly, and then pitch over on his back. He had only wounded him—got him in the gut, not the head. Cursing, weeping, Pratt fumbled with the bolt. He had failed; he had not killed him.

While he was trying to fire again, a vast gray shape loomed up, drew back its foot, and kicked the gun from his hands. Two more shapes appeared; he experienced a blossoming second of agony, and then it was over. His last instant of life had passed. Between the three of them, the gray toughs had decapitated him.

Sitting on the pavement, spitting blood, Jones sat waiting for the police medical teams to reach him. From where he squatted, he could see the remains of the assassin. Dimly, through a haze, he watched the infuriated gray figures destroy what was left.

It was over. Between his clenched fingers, the living warmth of his blood oozed. He had been wounded; but he was still alive. In his agony there was already the roaring joy of victory.

14

Pearson was sitting at his desk when the first reports came in. He listened idly; they seemed to come from a long way off, remote and theoretical, without immediate importance. He gave his acknowledgment and turned away from the relay.

After awhile it occurred to him that he had failed. Pratt was dead, and Jones lay groaning in a police hospital. Jones was still alive. Well, that was it.

Getting to his feet, he walked over to the window. Hands in his pockets, he stood gazing out at the dark, nocturnal city. Very little stirred. In the next day or so, police units would round up Jones' followers in this area. There was no hurry; it could wait. In fact, it could wait forever.

But he had to go through with it. All the way to the bitter end. He had started it; he had to finish it. He did not intend to back out now, simply because there was no hope.

He thought briefly of trying to murder Jones in the hospital, as he lay helpless. No, he had already made his quixotic gesture. He had already proven what he set out to prove, what he had to know.

Jones could not be killed. It was futile. Fedgov was through; he might as well throw in the sponge.

As a matter of fact, he waited two weeks. He waited until the actual figures on the plebiscite began to trickle in. He even procrastinated until the building reeked with the acrid fumes of burning paper: the official documents of Security going up in smoke. When the Supreme Council resigned, Pearson was still standing mutely in his Detroit office, head sunk down on his chest, hands in his pockets.

A few hours before the pale, weak figure of Jones rose from the hospital bed, entered an official car and headed toward Detroit, Pearson put in a call to Cussick.

"I'll come over there," Pearson told him. "I'll talk to you at your apartment; we're blowing up this building. We don't want to leave anything."

The first thhing he noticed as he entered Cussick's apartment was the general untidiness. He didn't remember it that way. For a moment he stood in the doorway, baffled and disturbed.

"That's right," he said finally. "Your wife's gone. You're here all alone."

Cussick closed the hall door. "Can I pour you a drink?"

"You bet your life," Pearson said gratefully. "A water high."

"I've got a fifth of good Scotch," Cussick said. He fixed the drinks, and the two of them sat down.

"We're through," Pearson said.

"I know."

"It was a mistake. Of course he couldn't be killed. But I had to try. You know, the son of a bitch might have been bluffing. It was an outside chance; I wanted to test him. Pragmatic, you know."

"What comes next?" Cussick asked. "Is there anything we haven't done?"

Pearson's hard, relentless face twisted. "As a matter of fact," he said slowly, "we have—technically—two more hours of authority. It'll take that long to make Jones the legal government. As of right now, I still have charge of Rafferty's project."

"Do you know what the project is? I thought you didn't know."

Glaring up at the ceiling, Pearson said: "There are two ships ready. I mean real ships, ships capable of space travel. You know what I mean. Interplan, they call them. Stored down in Ordnance somewhere, ready to go. They're kept on twenty-four-hour alert. Always ready. Always serviced and fueled." He added: "They're supposed to be the best. It's my understanding that they work by automatic beam. Somebody, I forget who, told me once that a pilot station on Venus controls them as soon as they leave Earth. Maybe it isn't Venus. Maybe it's Mars."

"Venus," Cussick affirmed.

Pearson nodded as he sipped his drink. "You realize, of course, that this is an elaborate little game. Naturally, I know what this project is; I found out the first day. But for the record, I'm talking only about the two ships. They—you understand who I mean—will be divided into two groups, four in one, four in the other. So if one ship fails to arrive, there'll be the other."

"On Venus," Cussick asked, "are there supplies? Some kind of installations?"

"Mountains of supplies. Miles of installations. All we have to do is get the eight of them there."

Cussick got to his feet. "I'll notify Rafferty.'

Pearson also rose. "My car's outside; I'll drive you to the field. Better yet, I'll come along."

Within half an hour they were setting down in San Francisco. Rafferty was asleep; Cussick roused him and delivered the message. Ordnance was notified. The transport Van was activated and the eight Venusians collected into it: seven adults and one baby still in its incubator. Frightened, bewildered, the mutants sat huddled together; timid persons, peering up, blinking rapidly, conversing in low, uncertain whispers.

"Good luck," Rafferty told them.

Pearson and Cussick rode along with the Van to Ordnance. They supervised the loading of the ships, four mutants in each. The complex safety seals were melted in place and the ships uprighted. As Cussick and Pearson and Rafferty watched from the shadows at the edge of the field, the ships were simultaneously launched. In all, the whole thing took an hour and a half: Jones still had thirty minutes to wait.

"Feel like a drink?" Cussick asked Pearson and Rafferty.

The three of them got thoroughly drunk. In their grim stupor, time and space ceased to have meaning. The world blurred in a chaotic swirl of drifting phantoms, indistinct sounds, shifting colors and shafts of light. Sometime during the process, an event momentarily caught Cussick's attention.

Four gray-uniformed men stood around them, examining their identification papers with brisk efficiency. Muddled, with a violent effort of will, he focussed on them.

"What do you want?" he demanded. But they weren't interested in him; it was Pearson they were grabbing hold of and carting off. Suddenly horrified, Cussick struggled furiously; in a frenzy he waded in and fought to save Pearson. One of the gray-uniformed figures shoved him down, and another stepped on his face.

Then they were gone. Cussick lay on the floor beside the inert shape of Rafferty, among overturned stools and broken glass. Gradually, reluctantly, the frigid gray of sanity crept back into his mind. Pearson had been arrested. Outside the bar boomed a growing cacophony of sounds: the roar of motors, shrieks, shouts, marching feet, exploding shells.

The remaining half hour had passed. Jones was in office. The day of the Crisis Government, the new world order, had begun.

15

In the cramped, low-ceilinged shop cabin, a small figure sat hunched over a workbench; soldering gun gripped in both hands, he moodily pondered a tangled mass of electronic parts and wiring. Except for the hum of the gun's coils the cabin was silent. Nothing stirred. The metal walls of the cabin were cold, smooth, impersonal. Storage compartments, stenciled with code numbers, covered every flat surface. No space had been wasted; the cabin was a square block of efficiency.

The transistors, relays, and heaps of wiring spread out on the bench formed the steering mechanism of a signal rocket. The signal rocket itself, six feet long and four inches in diameter, stood propped up in the corner, a thin metal skin minus its insides. Pasted on the wall behind the bench dangled greasy, crumpled schematics. Blue-white light flooded down from a flexible snake-lamp. Repair tools of every kind sparkled metallically.

"I can't do it," Louis said aloud, for his own benefit. Suddenly he began feverishly tearing wires loose and resoldering them in alternate combinations. For ten minutes, solder steamed and sizzled and activated the mechanism of the rocket. Tubes lit up; electricity moved through the circuit.

Nothing happened. In a flurry of activity, he again jerked leads loose, switched them at random, and resoldered them. Blowing and spitting on the cooling metal, poking at the smoking terminals, he watched anxiously as the circuit carried power one final time.

Still nothing.

He set the time switch for ninety seconds, the interval Dieter had computed. Tik-tok went the mechanism. Tik-tok, tik-tok, tik-tok, tik-tok until he couldn't stand it; cutting down the interval to five seconds he waited in a controlled hysteria until the relays snapped shut, and the clicking ceased.

His wristwatch told him it was still a second off. In ninety seconds it would be eighteen seconds off. Or worse; maybe it would never trip. Maybe the signal rocket would shoot past the other ship, out into the darkness, without ever releasing its magnetic pick-up grapple. The hell with it. He didn't know enough about electronics.

"I'm no good," he said, speaking in general, meaning himself and not merely what he had done. Meaning himself and his whole life. In the small shop cabin his voice squeaked back at him, a thin and brittle sound . . . but a sound, nevertheless. Any sound was welcome.

"You—" he said to the tangled remains on the bench, expressing himself from the bottom of his soul. There was nobody around to hear, so he thought of a few more terms and uttered them aloud. It sounded odd to hear his little voice bleating out obscenities. He was surprised, almost shocked. Rage vanished, and shame took its place.

"Irma could fix it," he said unhappily. And then he was overcome with fright. Pure, sheer, fright. Very quietly he closed his eyes and screamed. Like a man with something terrible caught in his throat, he sat stiffly at the workbench, fingers curled like talons, skin cold and clammy, tongue extended, shoulders hunched, mouth locked open, shrieking out the fear inside him.

And it wouldn't help, because they wouldn't hear him back on Earth anyhow. *I'm out here,* he was yelling. I'm trillions of miles out here, alone. There's nothing around me; I'm falling by myself, and nobody knows or gives a damn. Help me! Take me back! I want to go home!

And all the time he realized it was infantile stupidity, because, in fact, he was *not* alone: Dieter and Vivian and the baby, Laura, were along with him, plus a titanic metal ship as long as four city blocks, weighing thousands of tons, crammed with a billion dollars worth of turbines, safety devices, supplies. So it was all nonsense.

Trembling, he reached out and touched the wall. By God, it seemed real enough. What more could he ask? Could it get any more real? What would it look like if it were more real? His thoughts went around and around, without a flywheel, spinning crazily, faster and faster.

He crossed to the door, yanked it absolutely shut, bolted it, peered through the crack, and was satisfied. He was locked in; even if he went completely berserk, it would be all right: nobody would see him, nobody would know, there was no harm he could do. He could wreck the whole shop cabin, and it wouldn't make any difference. Not like running amuck outside, where he could get at the delicate automatic pilot.

The metal walls of the shop cabin had a bright, metallic quality. They looked like metalfoil, thin as paper, even thinner. A fragile metal hide between him and the emptiness. He could feel it out there; putting his hand against the wall, suffering incredibly but forcing himself, he stood actually *touching* the outside emptiness.

He could hear it. He could sense it, practically smell it. A cold musty smell, like moldy paper. A deserted trash heap blowing around at night; wind so faint that it was invisible, stirring so slightly that no motion was felt, only the sense of presence. It was always there, outside the ship. It never ceased.

Resentment took the place of fear. Why hadn't they fixed up communication between the two ships? And why hadn't they fixed up some sort of sound? There was no sound; the turbines were off—except for occasional shattering split seconds when side jets came on momentarily to correct the course. How did he know the ship was moving? He listened, but he heard nothing; he sniffed, he peered, he reached out his hand, but there wasn't anything there. Only the metalfoil wall, seemingly thinner than paper, so fragile that he could tear it to shreds.

On and on he pondered. Around and around. And all the time the ship and its invisible companion were getting nearer to Venus.

In the other ship, Frank was in the communications room, bent over the receiver.

"In the first seventy-two hours of the Crisis Government," the faint, static-laden voice of the Earth announcer stated, "there has already been a marked change in the people's morale."

Irma and Frank glanced at each other cynically.

"The previous apathy and futility that characterized life under the Fedgov system has vanished; the man in the street has a new zest, a new purpose in life. He now has confidence in his leaders; he knows that his leaders will act; he knows his leaders are not corrupted by intellectual paralysis."

"What's that mean?" Syd asked dryly.

"It means they act first and think second," Irma said.

The voice raved on. In the corner, the tape recorder was taking it all down. The four people listened avidly, not wanting to miss a word, loathing everything the voice said.

"It's so—silly," Irma said. "So sort of stupid and trashy,

like bad advertising. But they believe it; they take it seriously."

"The wheels are rolling," Garry stuttered. "Grinding it out. Swords sharpened cheap—hey, a new business. If we ever get back to Earth. Swords sharpened, armor polished, horses shod. Our slogan is: Everything in Medieval Equipment. If it's medieval, we have it."

Nobody was listening to him; the announcer had finished and the three adults were now sunk in gloomy thought.

"We're lucky," Frank said, after awhile. "If we were back there the People's Crusade Against the Invading Horde would be after us. We're not a horde, and we're not invading, but otherwise we fit pretty well."

"It's a good thing somebody thought to send us away," Syd observed. "Was it Rafferty's idea? That whole business at the end was so confused . . . I'm still not sure what happened."

"Rafferty was out there," Garry asserted. "I saw him hurrying around. He yelled something in at us, but I couldn't hear him."

"Obviously," Frank said, "they had all this set up; they didn't build these ships that morning. Somebody—probably Rafferty—planned to get us off Earth. That much we can assume. The real problem is: what the hell lies at the other end?"

"Maybe they just wanted to get rid of us," Irma said uneasily. "Sort of dump us out into space. A one-way trip."

"But," Syd pointed out, "if they just wanted to get rid of us, they could have done it years ago. Done it cheaply and easily, without going to all the trouble of building the Refuge, and these ships, all the equipment geared to our needs. It doesn't make sense."

"What's Venus like?" Irma asked Garry. "You read books—you know everything."

The boy flushed. "A barren waste. No air, no life."

"Are you sure?" Frank demanded, unconvinced.

"Arid wastes. No water. Dry dust blowing around. Deserts."

"You donkey," Frank said, disgusted. "That's Mars."

"What's the difference? Mars, Jupiter, Venus, Pluto . . . they're all the same."

"Are we going to live in a dome with the scout teams?" Syd wondered. "We can't; we'll have to have our own dome. A Refuge inside a Refuge."

"They should have told us," Garry complained.

"There wasn't time," Syd complained.

"Time, hell," Frank retorted. "They've had thirty years to tell us. All my life, year after year, and not one word."

"I'm sorry," Irma said, "but I can't see that it makes any difference. What's there to tell? We know where we're going. There's nothing we can do about it; we can't alter the course of the ships."

"The trouble with us," Syd said thoughtfully, "is that we're used to having things decided for us. We've never really done anything on our own. We're like children; we've never grown up."

"Our womb," Frank agreed. He indicated the ship. "And it's still around us."

"We let them think for us, make our plans. We just drift along, like now. We have no conception of responsibility."

"What else can we do?" Garry demanded.

"Nothing." Syd considered. "I wonder if it'll ever end. I wonder if a time will come when we're on our own, making our own plans."

Nobody said anything; nobody could imagine what it would be like.

The passage between Earth and Venus took two hundred eighty hours and forty-five minutes. Toward the last stages, when the misty greenish orb had risen and filled up the sky,

Frank sat alone in the communications room, hands clenched together, waiting.

The ship was no longer silent. All around him the floor and walls boomed with the din of braking jets. Automatic relays were responding to the planet; a spiraling course was being set that gradually lowered the ship toward the surface. In front of Frank, rows of lights lit up in shifting patterns: robot equipment was engaging itself in answer to the situation.

The audspeaker clicked, sizzled with static, and then spoke. "This is the service dome on Venus." A human voice, loud and very close, not more than a few thousand miles away. "Who are you? Why are you landing? We don't have any reports." The voice sounded hopeful, but skeptical. "Please describe yourselves. Supply ship? Replacements? Troupe of dancers?"

Another voice asked: "You bringing us more equipment? We're short as hell on food-processing machinery."

"Books," the first man said emphatically. "Christ, we're dying. What's all this stuff about Jones? Who the hell is Jones? Is all this on the level?"

"You have news?" the other man demanded eagerly. "Is it true they're sending ships out past Sirius? Whole flocks of them?"

Frank sat helpless; there was nothing he could do to answer. The transmitter, like everything else, was robot-controlled. It was terrible to hear the pleading voices, very close by, and not be able to respond.

And then the response came. At first he couldn't imagine where it originated. It boomed out deafeningly; the sound washed over his ears in shattering waves.

"This ship," the voice thundered, "is robot-directed. Its passengers have no control over it. The ship and its companion are under the protection of Fedgov."

It was Doctor Rafferty's voice. The voice, taped and incorporated into the automatic equipment of the ship, was issuing from the bank of lights directly above his head. An old tape, prepared when there was still a Fedgov, when the term still meant something.

"This ship," Rafferty explained, "will guide itself to the restricted installation in the N-area of the planet. The companion ship, also robot-controlled, will follow after an interval of one hour. It is requested that you give the passengers as much cooperation as possible, especially in the event that unforeseen difficulties occur." He added: "This is a taped explanation by a legal representative of Fedgov. It will be repeated until the landing takes place."

The weaker voices returned, full of astonishment. "It's them!" one hollered thinly. "Get the ambulances over to N! They're coming down on automatic!"

Scrambling sounds, and the Venus transmitter clicked off. Now there was only static until, five minutes later, Rafferty's statement thunderously repeated itself.

It continued, spaced by five-minute breaks, until the emergency jets screamed it aside, and the ship plunged into the thick lower bands of atmosphere that enclosed the planet.

Stumbling in his haste, Frank made his way out of the communications room, down the corridor to the lounge. The lounge was empty; the others had left it. Terrified, he raced around in a half-circle, yelling into the uproar. The ship was animate with sound, a screeching organic racket, as if every molecule had grown a mouth and was shrieking out its pain.

Garry appeared and grabbed hold of his arm; he was shouting, but nothing came out: only gestures and mouth-motions. Frank followed along; Garry led him to an interior chamber, a reinforced cell at the heart of the ship. Irma and Syd stood mutely together, eyes wide, skins pale with shock. The chamber was the miniature medical ward of the ship. They had retreated here instinctively, pulling as far into safety as possible.

Now the brake jets had cut off. Either the ship was out of fuel, or it was deliberately coasting. Frank wondered about the other ship; he thought about Louis and Vivian and Dieter and the baby. He wished they could be together, all eight of them. He wished—

The impact wiped out his thoughts. And for a long time, how long he never knew, there was simple nothingness; no world and no self, only empty nonexistence. Not even the awareness of pain.

The first sensation that returned was that of weight. He was lying in the corner, and his head was ringing. Clanging like a great church bell, and slowly wheeling around, his head drifted sickeningly. The chamber was a shambles, crumpled in as if some Behemoth had trod on it. At one point, the ceiling and the floor met. Pools of liquid, probably insulating fluid, poured from broken wall-pipes. Somewhere in the half-darkness a mechanical repair car was ludicrously fussing with a rent in the hull as large as a two-story house.

Well, that was it. The ship had been ripped open like an over-inflated bladder. A dense, fragrant, steaming fog was already billowing in from outside. The ambulances would arrive to find them dead.

"Frank," Garry whispered.

Frank struggled up. Syd lay crumpled; probably she was dead. He felt her pulse. No, she was alive. He and Garry stumbled through the ruins of the chamber, toward what had been the passage. The passage was sealed off by a collapsed wall; the only exit was the rip in the hull. They could go only one way: out. Around them, the ship was flattened junk.

"Where's Irma?" Frank demanded hoarsely.

Garry was shoving through heaps of debris, toward the rip. "Out. She crawled out." Grunting, struggling, he disappeared into the swirls of moist fog, and dropped through the rip. Frank followed.

The scene was unbelievable. For a time neither of them

could grasp it. "We're back home," the boy murmured, dazed and confused. "Something went wrong. We went around in a circle."

But it wasn't the Refuge. And yet it *was*. Familiar hazy hills spread out, lost in billowing moisture. Green lichens grew everywhere; the soil was a tangled floor of lush growing plants. The air smelled of intricate organic life, a rich, complex odor, similar to the odor they remembered but, at the same time, far more alive. They gaped foolishly: there was no delineating wall. There was no finite hull confining it. The world lay stretched out as far as the eye could see. And above. The world was everywhere.

"My God," Frank said. "It's not a fake." Bending down, he snatched up a crawling snail-like insect. "Not a robot— this is alive. It's genuine!"

From the mist, Irma appeared. Blood oozed over one eye; her hair was matted and tangled, her clothing was torn. "We're home," she gasped, gripping a bulging armload of plant life she had gathered. "Look at it—remember it? And we can *breathe*. We can live."

Off in the distance, great columns of steam rose up, geysers of boiling water forced through the rocks to the surface. An immense ocean pounded somewhere, invisible in the drifting curtain of moisture.

"Listen," Frank said. "You hear that? You hear the water?"

They listened. They heard. They reached down and felt; they threw themselves on the ground, clutching frantically, faces pressed to the damp, warm soil.

"We're home," Irma wept. All of them were crying and moaning, wailing in bewildered joy. And above them, the other ship was already thundering down.

16

Under its cloud layer the surface temperature of Venus varied from 99 degrees Fahrenheit to 101 degrees Fahrenheit. The lower atmosphere was a mixture of ammonia and oxygen, heavily laden with water vapor. Among the oceans and rolling hills toiled a variety of life-forms, building and evolving, planning and creating.

Louis and Irma were repairing a turbine-driven tractor, when Dieter excitedly put in his appearance. "It's ready!" he shouted, standing in the entrance of the shed. "We're going to start!"

From under the tractor, Louis stuck out his head. "What's ready?" he demanded sourly.

"The corn. We're going to harvest it. We've got all the equipment down there; Vivian's hooking it up." Dieter danced up and down with frenzy. "You all have to pitch in— this stuff can wait. I rounded up Frank and Syd; they're on their way. They'll meet us along the route. And Garry's tagging along."

Grumbling, Louis dragged himself out from under the tractor. "It isn't corn. Stop calling it corn."

"It's corn in the spiritual sense. It's the *essence* of corn."

"Even if it's dark green?" Irma asked, amused.

"Even if it's purple-striped and silver polka-dotted. Even if it stands ninety feet high and has lace-embroidered pods. Even if it spurts ambrosia and coffee-grounds. It's still corn."

Louis stood wiping his forehead. "We can't come until the tractor's working." It was fifty miles to Dieter's place, across rolling country. "I think we need a new ignition coil; that means back to the ship."

"The heck with it," Dieter said impatiently, "I've got my dobbin cart—we can all fit in that."

The dobbin cart and the dobbin itself waited quietly. Louis approached cautiously, his eyes narrow with suspicion. "What do you call it?" He had seen the animals a long way off, but never this close. The dobbin was mostly legs, with immense flat feet like leather suction cups. A matted pelt, ragged and uneven, hung over it. The dobbin's head was tiny; its eyes were half-shut and indolent. "How'd you trap it?" he asked.

"They're tame enough, if you have the patience." Dieter climbed up into the cart and grabbed hold of the reins. "I've taught the hell out of this thing. They're sort of quasi-telepathic; all I have to do is think what I want, and off it goes." He wrinkled his nose contemptuously. "Forget that tractor; you can't keep it running anyhow. This is the vehicle of the future—the dobbin cart is the coming thing."

Irma got gingerly into the cart beside Dieter, and after a moment Louis followed. The car was crude but solid; Dieter had laboriously constructed it during the last four months. The material was a now-familiar, heavy bread-like plant fiber that rapidly hardened on exposure. After it had been aged and dried, it could be cut, sawed, polished, and stained. Occasionally, migratory animals gnawed the material away, but that was the only known hazard.

The dobbin's vast flat feet began rhythmically to pound; the cart moved forward. Behind them, Louis' cabin dwindled. He and Irma had single-handedly built it; a year had passed in which much had been accomplished. The cabin, made of the same bread-like substance, was surrounded by acres of cultivated land. The so-called *corn* grew in dense clumps; it wasn't really corn, but it functioned as corn. Bulging pods ripened in the moist atmosphere. Around the base of the crop, insects crept; predators devouring plant-pests. The fields were irrigated by shallow trenches bringing water out of an underground spring that spilled up to the surface in a hot, bubbling torrent. In the warm, humid atmosphere, almost unchanging, virtually hothouse in its stability, four crops a year were possible.

Parked in front of the cabin were half-assembled machines carted from the wreckage of the ships. Gradually, Irma was reconstructing new implements from the remains of the old. The fuel pipes of the ships were now sewage drains. The control board wiring carried electricity from the water-driven generator to the cabin.

Standing glumly in the shed beyond the cabin were a variety of indigenous herbivores, drowsily munching moist hay. A number of species had been collected; it wasn't yet established what each was good for. Already, ten types with edible flesh had been catalogued, plus two types secreting drinkable fluids. A gargantuan beast covered with thick hair served as a source of muscle-power. And now the big-footed dobbin that Dieter used to pull his cart.

The dobbin raced determinedly down the road; in a matter of seconds it had hit full velocity. Feet flying, it sped like a furry ostrich, tiny head erect, legs a blur of motion. Blop-blop was the noise a running dobbin made. The cart bounced wildly; Louis and Irma held on for their lives. Delirious with joy, Dieter clutched the reins and urged the thing faster.

"This is fast enough," Irma managed, gritting her teeth.

"You haven't seen anything," Dieter yelled. "This thing really loves to run."

A wide ditch lay ahead, a tumble of rocks and shrubs. Louis closed his eyes; the car was already on the verge of bursting apart. "We won't make it," he grunted. "We'll never get across."

As it reached the ditch, the dobbin unfolded two stubby, rattyhided wings and flapped them energetically. The dobbin and the cart rose slightly in the air, hung over the ditch, and then bumpily lowered on the far side.

"It's a bird," Irma gasped.

"Yes!" Dieter shouted. "It can go anywhere. That's my good dobbin." He leaned precariously forward and whacked the thing on its shaggy rump. "Noble dobbin! Majestic bird!"

The landscape shot past. To the far right rose a hazy range of mountains, mostly lost in the drifting swirls of fog that kept the surface of the planet always damp. A solid skin of growing vegetation and creeping insects . . . everywhere Louis looked there was life. Except at one charred spot at the base of the mountains, a black sore already beginning to turn green as plant-life quietly covered it.

The scout domes had been there. The non-Venusians who had preceded them, cooped up in their "refuges," their airtight stations. Now they were dead; only the eight Venusians remained.

When the second ship had landed, the ambulances were already on the way. The second landing was more successful; nobody had been hurt, and the ship was virtually undamaged. The ambulances had collected the injured and taken them to the installations set up in anticipation of their arrival. During the first month, the non-Venusians had cooperated fully—in spite of orders from the Crisis Government. Then, toward March, the Crisis Government had stopped transmitting. A week later a heavy-duty projectile had come bursting down on the non-Venusian domes; within a day only the eight Venusians were extant.

The death of the non-Venusians was a shock, but a shock they could recover from. The problem of their own existence was simplified; now they were totally on their own, without communication of any sort with non-Venusians.

Between the ruined domes and their own ships and installations there was ample intact equipment at their disposal. Promptly, they had begun carting it off and putting it into operation. But a lethargy crept over them. Finally they had ceased the regular pilgrimages; they stopped collecting the Earth-manufactured materials, the elaborate machinery and industrial products.

None of them really wanted to go on from the point at which they had left off. In actuality they wanted to start from the bottom up. It was not a replica of Earth-civilization that they wanted to create; it was their own typical community, geared to their own unique needs, geared to the Venusian conditions, that they wanted.

It had to be agrarian.

They already had crops and simple cabins, irrigation ditches, clothing woven from plant fiber, electricity, a pair of dobbin-drawn carts, sanitation and wells. They had domesticated native animals; they had located natural building materials. They were shaping basic tools and functional artifacts. In their first year, thousands of years of cultural evolution had been achieved. Perhaps, in a decade—

Off beyond the meadow was a long gully. Occasional drifters lay here and there among the shubbery; a cloud had come settling down, the week before. And beyond the gully, in the shadows of a wide ridge, rested an immense wad of white material.

"What's that?" Dieter inquired, interrupting Louis' thoughts. "I've never seen that life-form."

In the second dobbin cart, Frank and Syd approached. The

Venusians gathered silently, uneasy in the presence of the ominous mound of white. In Syd's arms the baby stirred fitfully.

"It doesn't belong here," Frank said finally.

"Why do you say that?" Dieter asked. "Who are you to pass judgment?"

"I mean," Frank explained, "it's not Venusian. It came down a day or so after the drifters."

"Came down!" Dieter was perplexed. "What do you mean?"

Frank shrugged. "Like the drifters. It descended."

"I saw another one," Irma volunteered. "Apparently it's a second interstellar life-form."

Abruptly, Louis' hand closed around Dieter's shoulder. "Take the cart over to it. I want to examine it."

Dieter's face sagged resentfully. "Why? I want to show you my corn."

"The hell with your corn," Louis said sharply. "We better take a look at that thing."

"I looked at the other one," Frank said. "It seemed harmless. I couldn't see any special characteristics . . . it's a single cell, like the drifters." He hesitated. "I broke it open. It's got a nucleus, cell-wall, granules within the cytoplast. The usual stuff; it's definitely a protozoon."

Dieter headed the dobbin cart toward the wad of white. In a moment they had drawn up beside it and halted. The other cart followed. One of the dobbins sniffed at the white wad; without comment he began to nibble.

"Leave that alone," Dieter ordered nervously. "Maybe it'll poison you."

Louis leaped down and strode over.

The wad was faintly moist. It was alive, all right. Louis got a stick and began prodding it experimentally. Here was a second life-form out of space, a rarer form, not as common as the smaller drifters. "Just two?" he asked. "Nobody's seen any more?"

"There's one over there," Irma said, pointing.

A quarter of a mile away a third wad had recently landed. From where they stood they could see it sluggishly stirring . . . the wad was making its way slowly over the ground. Its movement slowed. Presently it came to rest.

"It's dead," Dieter commented indifferently.

Louis walked over toward it, across the spongy green surface of plant life. Tiny animals scuttled underfoot, hardshelled crustaceans. He ignored them and kept his eyes on the looming wad of white. When he reached it, he discovered that it wasn't dead; it had found a hollow depression and was laboriously anchoring itself. Fascinated, he watched it exude a slimy cement. The cement hardened, and the wad was tightly fixed to the ground. There it rested, obviously waiting.

Waiting for what?

Curious, he walked all around it. The surface was uniform. It certainly looked like a cell, all right: a giant single cell. He picked up a rock and tossed it; the rock embedded itself in the white substance and stuck there.

No doubt it was related to the drifters. Two stages, perhaps; that was the probable explanation. The drifters, he knew, were incomplete; they lacked the ability to ingest food, to reproduce, even to stay alive. But this thing was clearly staying alive: it was getting itself set up. A symbiotic relationship, perhaps?

While he was studying it, he noticed the drifter.

The drifter was coming down. He had seen it happen before, but it always fascinated him. The drifter was using the air as a medium: carefully it maneuvered itself like a weedspore, first floating in one direction, then in another, keeping itself aloft as long as possible. The drifters didn't like to land; it meant an end to mobility.

There it came, drifting down to its death, to expire fruitlessly. The senseless mystery of the interstellar creature: wandering millions, billions of miles, over centuries—for what? To wind up here, to perish without purpose?

The familiar cosmic meaninglessness. Life without goal. In the last two years billions of drifters had been exterminated. It was tragic, stupid. This one, hovering momentarily, was trying to keep itself alive one last second, before it fell to its pointless death. A hopeless struggle; like all of its race, it was doomed.

Suddenly the drifter folded into itself. Its thin, extended body snapped together like a rubber band; one second it was spread out, catching air currents—the next second it was a thin elongated pencil. It had literally rolled itself up in a tube. And now, thin and tube-like, it dropped straight down.

The tube-like projectile fell expertly, purposefully, directly into the wad of white dough.

It neatly penetrated the white wad. The surface closed after it, and no sign of it remained.

"It's a house," Dieter said uncertainly. "That's a dwelling, and the drifter lives in it."

The white mass had begun to change. Incredulous, Louis saw it swell until it was almost double its original size. It couldn't be; it was impossible. But even as he stood there, the wad divided into two hemispheres, joined, but clearly distinct. Rapidly, the white mass grew and formed four connecting units. Now growth was frantic; the thing bubbled and swelled like yeast. Two, four, eight, sixteen . . . geometric progression.

A chill, ominous wind eddied around him. The undulating shape seemed to cut off the sunlight; all at once he was standing in a darkening shadow. In panic, Louis retreated. His terror spread to the two dobbins; as he reached out to take hold of Dieter's cart the birds suddenly unfolded their wings and bolted. Dragging the carts after them, they floundered away from the swelling white shape. He was left standing alone, impotent and stunned.

"What is it?" Frank was shouting. Hysteria rose up into his voice; now they were all yelling. "What is it? What's happening?"

Dieter leaped to the ground and stood with his feet braced apart, the reins gripped. "Come on," he shout to Louis. "Get in!"

With a snarl of aversion, the dobbin shuddered away from Louis. Ignoring it, he clambered into the cart and sat hunched over, lips moving, face white. Dieter leaped back in, and the cart began to move away.

"It's an egg," Syd said faintly.

"Was," Louis corrected. "Not now. Now it's a zygote."

The cosmic egg had been fertilized by the microgametophyte. And Louis, watching, knew what the drifters were.

"Pollen," he whispered, stricken. "That's what they've been all the time. And we never guessed."

The drifters were pollen, radiating in clouds across space between star systems, in search of their megagametophytes. Neither they nor the white wad was the final organism; both were elements of the now visibly growing embryo.

And he realized something else. Nobody had guessed, but Jones must have known this—and for some time.

The team of biologists spread out their reports. Jones barely glanced at the collection of papers; he nodded and moved away, deep in brooding thought.

"We were afraid that might be it," Trillby, the head of the team, said. "That explains their incompleteness; that's why they don't have digestive or reproductive systems." He added, "They *are* a reproductive system. Half of it, at least."

"What's the word?" Jones asked suddenly. "I forget."

"Metazoon. Multi-celled. Differentiated into various organs and special tissues."

"And we haven't seen the final stages?"

"God, no," Trillby said emphatically. "Nothing like it. The organism uses the planet as a womb; the most we've observed is the embryo and what might correspond to the fetal stage. At that point, it bursts off the planet. The atmosphere, the gravitational field, are a medium for early development; after that it's through with us. I suppose the final organism is nonplanetary."

"It lives between systems?" Jones inquired, frowning. His face was wrinkled and preoccupied; he only half-heard the man. "It breeds on planets . . . sheltered places."

Trillby said: "We have reason to believe that all the so-called drifters are pollen grains from a single adult plant—if those terms have any meaning. Maybe it's neither plant nor animal. A combination of both . . . a plant's immobility and using a plant's method of pollination."

"Plants," Jones said. "They don't fight. They're helpless."

"Generally speaking. But we shouldn't assume that these—"

Jones nodded absently. "Of course . . . it's absurd. We can't really know anything about them." Wearily, he rubbed his forehead. "I'll keep your report here. Thanks."

He left them standing there, surrounding their report like a cluster of anxious hens. Offices danced past him, and then he was out in the barren, drafty corridor that connected the administrative wing with the police wing. Glancing at his pocket watch he saw that it was almost time. *Time*. Infuriated, he stuffed the watch away, hating to see its placid, contemptuous face.

For one year, he had mulled the report over in his mind. He had memorized it word for word—and then sent out the team to collect it. They had done a good job: it was an exhaustive study.

From outside the building came sounds. Shuddering, Jones halted, aware of them in a vague way, conscious that the unending murmur was still there. Shakily, he ran his fingers through his hair, smoothing it back as best he could. Putting himself in some semblance of order.

He was a plain little man with steel-rimmed glasses and thinning hair. He wore a simple gray uniform, with a single medal on his sunken chest, plus the regulation crossed-flasks armband. His life was an endless procession of work. He had a duodenal ulcer from tension and worry. He was conscientious.

He was licked.

But the crowd outside didn't know that. Outside the building, it had grown to monumental size. Thousands of people, collected together in an excited clot, yelling and waving their arms, cheering, holding up banners and signs. The noise drifted and eddied, a distant booming that had been going on—with few respites—for over a year. There was always somebody outside the building, screeching his head off. Idly, Jones considered the various slogans; in an automatic, almost bureaucratic way, he checked them against the program he had laid out.

WE HAVE FAITH
NOT YET BUT NOT LONG
JONES KNOWS—JONES DOES

Jones knew, all right. Grimly, he paced around in a circle, arms folded, impatient and restless. Eventually, after tramping down the hedges around the police building, the crowd would disperse. Still cheering, still shouting slogans at one another, they would drift off. The organization die-hards would go take ice-cold showers, would return to their various posts to plot the next stage of the grand strategy. None of them realized it yet: the Crusade was over. In a few days the ships would be coming back.

At the far end of the corridor a door was pushed aside;

two men appeared, Pearson and an armed, gray-uniformed guard. Pearson came toward him, a tall, thin man, pale, with tight-set lips. He showed no surprise at the sight of Jones; coming almost up to him, he halted, scrutinized the smaller man, glanced around at the armed guard behind him, and shrugged.

"It's been a long time," Pearson said. He moistened his lips. "I haven't seen you since that day we first picked you up."

"A lot has changed," Jones said. "Have you been well-treated?"

"I've been in a cell for just about a year," Pearson answered mildly, without rancor, "if you call that being well-treated."

"Bring in two chairs," Jones ordered the guard. "So we can sit down." When the guard hesitated, Jones flushed and shouted: "Do as I say—everything's under control."

The chairs were lugged back; without preamble, Jones seated himself. Pearson did the same.

"What do you want?" Pearson demanded bluntly.

"You've heard about the Crusade?"

Pearson nodded. "I've heard."

"What are your feelings?"

"I think it's a waste of time."

Jones considered. "Yes," he agreed. "It is a waste of time."

Astonished, Pearson started to speak, then changed his mind.

"The Crusade is over," Jones stated. "It failed. I'm informed that what we call *drifters* are the pollen of immensely complicated plant-like beings, so remote and advanced that we'll never have anything more than a dim picture of them."

Pearson sat staring at him. "You mean that?"

"I certainly do."

"Then we're a—" He gestured. "What are we? Nothing!"

"That's a good way of putting it."

"Maybe they think we're a chemical."

"Or a virus. Something on that order. On that scale."

"But—" Haltingly, Pearson demanded: "What are they going to do? If we've been attacking their pollen, destroying their spores—"

"The final adult forms have a direct, rational solution. Very shortly they'll move to protect themselves. I can't blame them."

"They're going to—eliminate us?"

"No, they're going to seal us off. A ring will presently be set up around us. We'll have Earth, the Sol System, the stars we've already reached. And that's all. Beyond that—" Jones snapped his fingers. "The warships will simply disappear. The blight or virus or chemical is contained. Bottled up inside a sanitary barrier. An effective solution: no wasted motions. A clean, straight-to-the point answer. Characteristic of their plant-like form."

Pearson pulled himself upright. "How long have you known this?"

"Not long enough. The war had already begun. If there had been spectacular interstellar battles"—Jones' voice died to a baffled, almost inaudible whisper—"people might have been satisfied. *Even if we had lost*, at least there would be glory, struggle, an adversary to hate. But there's nothing. In a few days the ring will be installed and the ships will have to turn back. Not even defeat. Just emptiness."

"What about them?" Pearson pointed toward the window, beyond which the noisy crowd cheered on. "Can they stand hearing it?"

"I did my best," Jones said levelly. "I bluffed and I lost. I had no idea what we were attacking. I was in the dark."

"We should have been able to guess," Pearson said.

"I don't see why. You find it easy to imagine?"

"No," Pearson admitted. "No, it's difficult."

"You used to be Director of the Secpol," Jones said. "When I came into power I had the Security setup disbanded and atomized. The structure is gone—the camps are closed. Enthusiasm has kept us unified. But there won't be any more enthusiasm."

Sick fear settled over Pearson. "What the hell is this?"

"I'm offering you your job back. You can have your badge and desk again. And your title: Security Director. Your secret police, your weapons-police. Everything the way you had it . . . with only one change. The Fedgov Supreme Council will stay dissolved."

"And you'll have ultimate authority?"

"Naturally."

"Go jump in the creek."

Jones signalled the guard. "Send in Doctor Manion."

Doctor Manion was a bald, heavy-set individual in a spanking white uniform, nails manicured, hair faintly perfumed, lips thick and moist. He clutched a heavy metal box, which he laid gingerly on the table.

"Doctor Manion," Jones said, "this is Mr. Pearson."

Reflexively, the two men shook hands; Pearson stood rigid as Manion rolled up his sleeves, glanced at Jones, and then began opening the steel box. "I have it here," he confided. "It's in perfect shape; survived the trip beautifully." With pride, he added: "It's the finest specimen obtained, so far."

"Doctor Manion," Jones said, "is a research parasitologist."

"Yes," Manion quickly agreed, moon-like face flushed with professional eagerness. "You see, Mr.—Pearson? Yes, you see, Pearson, as you probably realize, one of our big problems was screening returning ships to make sure they didn't pick up parasitic organisms of a non-Terran nature. We didn't want to admit new forms of pathogenic"—he snapped open the box—"Organisms."

In the box lay a curled-up intestine of spongy gray organic material. The coil of living tissue was surrounded by a transparent capsule of gelatine. Very slightly, the creature stirred; its blind, eyeless tip moved, felt about, pressed itself to the surface with a damp sucker. It might have been a worm; its segmented sections undulated in a wave of sluggish activity.

"It's hungry," Manion explained. "Now, this isn't a direct parasite; it won't destroy its host. There'll be a symbiotic relationship until it's laid its eggs. Then the larvae will use the host as a source of nourishment." Almost fondly, he continued: "It resembles some of our own wasps. The full course of growth and egg-laying takes about four months. Now, our problem is this: we know how it lives on its own world—it's a native of the fifth Alphan planet, by the way. We've seen it operate within its customary host. And we've been able to introduce it into large-bodied Terran mammals, such as the cow, the horse, with varying results."

"What Manion wants to find out," Jones said, "is whether this parasite will stay alive in a human body."

"Growth is slow," Manion bubbled excitedly. "We only have to observe it once a week. By the time the eggs are laid, we'll know if it can adapt itself to a human. But as yet, we haven't been able to obtain a volunteer."

There was silence.

"Do you feel like volunteering?" Jones asked Pearson. "You have your choice; take one job or the other. If I were you, I'd prefer the one I was used to. You were an excellent cop."

"How can you do this?" Pearson said weakly.

"I have to," Jones answered. "I've got to have the police back. The secret-service has to be re-created, by people who are experts."

"No," Pearson said hoarsely. "I'm not interested. I won't have anything to do with it."

Doctor Manion was delighted. Trying to contain himself, he began fussing with the gelatine capsule. "Then we can go ahead?" To Pearson he revealed: "We can use the surgical labs here in this building. I've had opportunity to inspect them, and they're superb. I'm anxious to introduce this organism before the poor thing starves."

"That would be a shame," Jones acknowledged. "All the way from Alpha for nothing." He stood toying with the sleeve of his coat, while he pondered. Both Pearson and Manion watched him fixedly. Suddenly Jones said to the doctor: "You have a cigarette lighter?"

Mystified, Manion dug out a heavy gold lighter and passed it to him. Jones removed the plug and drizzled fluid onto the gelatine capsule. At that, Manion's face lost its smug optimism. "Good God—" he began, agitated. "What the hell—"

Jones ignited the fluid. Stunned, helpless, Manion had to stand there as the fluid, the capsule, and the organism within, blazed up in an acrid flicker of orange fire. Gradually the contents cooled to a black, bubbling slime.

"Why?" Manion protested weakly, not comprehending.

"I'm a provincial," Jones explained briefly. "Strange things, foreign things, make me sick."

"But—"

He handed Manion back his lighter. "You make me sicker. Take your box and get out of here."

Dazed, overwhelmed by the catastrophe, Manion gathered up the cooling metal box and stumbled off. The guard stepped aside, and he vanished through the door.

Breathing more easily, Pearson said: "You wouldn't co-operate with us. Kaminski wanted you to help Reconstruction."

"All right." Jones nodded curtly to the guard. "Take this man back to his cell. Keep him there."

"How long?" the guard inquired.

"As long as you can," Jones answered, with bitterness.

• • •

On the trip back to organizational headquarters, Jones sat bleakly meditating.

Well, he had expected to fail, hadn't he? Hadn't he known that Pearson would refuse? Hadn't he previewed the whole miserable episode, known he couldn't go through with the torture? He could—and would—say he had done it; but that didn't change the facts.

He was on his way out. There was a terrible, brutal time left to him, and nothing more. What he did now was desperate; it was ruthless and it was final. It was something people were going to discuss for centuries to come. But, frantic as it was, it was still basically and undeniably his death.

He had no certain knowledge of what was to become of society because he would not be around to see it. Very shortly, he would die. He had been contemplating it for almost a year; it could be ignored temporarily, but always it returned, each time more terrible and imminent.

After death, his body and brain would erode. And that was the hideous part: not the sudden instant of torment that would come in the moment of execution. That, he could bear. But not the slow, gradual disintegration.

A spark of identity would linger in the brain for months. A dim flicker of consciousness would persist: that was his future memory; that was what the wave showed him. Darkness, the emptiness of death. And, hanging in the void, the still-living personality.

Deterioration would begin at the uppermost levels. First, the highest faculties, the most cognizant, the most alert processes, would fade. An hour after death the personality would be animal. A week after, it would be stripped to a vegetable layer. The personality would devolve back the way it had come; as it had struggled up through the billions of years, so it would go back, step by step, from man to ape to early primate to lizard to frog to fish to crustacean to trilobite to protozoon. And after that: to mineral extinction. Final merciful end. But it would take time.

Normally, the devolving personality would not be aware, would not be conscious of the process. But Jones was unique. Now, at this moment, with his full faculties intact, he was experiencing it. Simultaneously, he was fully conscious, totally in possession of his senses—and at the same time he was undergoing ultimate psychic degeneration.

It was bearing. But he had to bear it. And every day, every week, it grew worse—until finally he would in actuality die. And then, thank God, the ordeal would end.

The suffering he had caused others did not compare with that which *he* had to undergo. But it was right; he deserved it. This was his punishment. He had sinned, and retribution had come.

The final, somber phase of Jones' existence had begun.

17

Cussick was deep in conversation with two members of the police resistance when the long black organization car pulled to a stop in front of the apartment building.

"Holy cow," one of the cops said softly, as he groped inside his coat. "What are they doing here?"

Cussick clicked off the lights; the living room dropped into instant darkness. There were two figures in the organization car. It was an official car: the crossed-flasks emblem was neatly stenciled on the doors and hood. For a moment the figures sat, not moving, not stirring. They were obviously talking.

"We can handle them," one of the cops said nervously, from behind Cussick. "There're three of us."

Disgusted, his companion said: "This is only their front block. They're probably on the roof and up the stairs."

Rigid and apprehensive, Cussick continued to watch. In the faint light of the midnight street, one of the two seated figures looked familiar. A car spun past, and, momentarily, the figures were outlined. An aching tautness crept through his heart: he was right. For what seemed like hours the two figures remained in the car. Then the door slid open. The familiar figure stepped to the sidewalk.

"A woman," one of the cops said wonderingly.

The figure slammed the car door, turned on her heel, and started at a brisk trot toward the entrance of the apartment house.

In a hoarse, unsteady voice, Cussick said: "You two clear out. I'll take care of this alone."

They gaped at him foolishly. Then the sight of their surprised faces was cut off: Cussick had pulled open the hall door and was racing down the thick-carpeted corridor to meet her.

She was on the stairs when she saw him coming. There she halted, gazing up, breathing rapidly, holding onto the bannister. She wore the severe gray suit of the organization, the little cap on her heavy blonde hair. But it was she; it was Nina. For an interval the two of them stood, Cussick at the top of the stairs, Nina below him, eyes bright, lips apart, nostrils dilated. Then she let go of the bannister and scampered up the rest of the way. A brief instant as her arms reached up for him hungrily, and then he had descended his own two steps to meet her. After that an indefinite time of holding her tight, feeling her against him, smelling the warm scent of her hair; taking in, after so many months, the smooth pressure of her body, the yearning, fervent need of her.

"Oof," she gasped finally. "You're going to break me."

He led her upstairs, still holding tightly onto her, not letting her go until they were inside the deserted apartment and the door had been locked behind them.

Glancing breathlessly around, Nina stood stripping off her gloves. He could see how nervous she was; her hands shook as she mechanically pushed the gloves into her purse. "Well?" she asked huskily. "How've you been?"

"Fine." He walked a little way off to have a good view of her. Under his gaze she faltered visibly; she shrank back against the wall, half-lifted her fingers to her throat, smiled, gazed appealingly up at him like an animal that had failed to show up for its dinner.

"Can I come back?" she asked, in a whisper.

"Back?" He was afraid to imagine what she meant.

Tears filled her eyes. "Guess not."

"Of course you can come back." He moved up and took hold of her. "You know you can come back. Any time. Any time you want."

"You better let go of me," she whispered. "I'm going to start weeping. Let me get out my handkerchief."

He let go reluctantly; with awkward fingers she got out her bit of handkerchief and blew her nose. For a moment she stood dabbing at her eyes, red lips twitching, not speaking or looking at him, just standing there in her gray organization uniform, trying not to cry.

"The son of a bitch," she said finally, in a thin, weak voice.

"Jones?"

"I'll tell you . . . when I can." Balling her handkerchief up, she began striding around the room, arms folded, chin up, face quivering. "Well, it's a long and not very pleasant story. I've been with the organization—I guess over two years, now."

"Twenty-eight months," he informed her.

"That sounds right." She turned suddenly to him. "It's over. I'm through."

"What happened?"

Nina felt in her pockets. "Cigarette?"

He got out his pack, lit a cigarette for her, and put it between her trembling lips.

"Thanks," she said, breathing swift jets of gray-blue smoke out into the room. "First, I think we better get out of here. He may pick you up—he's picking everybody up."

"But I've been cleared," Cussick protested.

"Darling, that makes no damn difference. You've heard

what he did to Pearson? No, I suppose not." Briskly taking hold of his arm she propelled him toward the door. "We'd be a lot safer out of here; take me somewhere, anywhere." Shivering, she stood up on her toes to kiss him briefly. "Something has happened. We—the organization—know it, now; Jones told us. Tomorrow morning the public will know."

"What is it?"

"The great Crusade is over. The ships are coming back. It's the end of Jones, the end of the organization. *Movement*, I mean. Now that we're in, we're supposed to call—"

Cussick found the doorknob. "That's wonderful," he managed.

"Wonderful?" She laughed brittlely. "It's terrible, darling. As soon as we're out of here, I'll tell you why."

He found an all-night beanery on a side street, two miles from his apartment. At the counter, a pair of drowsy patrons sat slumped over their coffee, listlessly reading newspapers. The waitress was perched in the back by the cooking controls, staring out at the night. In the corner a tune-maker ground out cadences to itself.

"Fine," Nina said, sliding into a booth at the rear of the cafe. "There's a back door, isn't there?"

Cussick located a back door behind the cooking equipment: the service and maintenance entrance. "What do you want to chew on?"

"Just coffee."

He got the two coffees, and for a time they sat stirring and meditating, glancing furtively at each other.

"You're looking pretty nice," he told her haltingly.

"Thank you. I sort of hoped I'd lost a pound or two."

"Do you mean this? You're going to stay?" He had to be sure. "You're not going off again?"

"I mean it," she answered simply, her eyes blue and direct. "Tomorrow morning I want to go and get Jackie." She added:

"I've been seeing him every once in a while. I've kept sort of control over him."

"Me, too," Cussick said.

As she sipped her coffee, Nina explained to him what had happened. In short, terse words she outlined the background on the drifters, and the situation with the mobile war units.

"The ring is up, now," she told him. "The ships are turning back, returning to Earth. Why not? There's nothing else they can do. Commander Ascott's flagship, that great big thing, will be the first one to land. Right now they're clearing the New York field."

"Pollen," Cussick said, stricken. "That explains their incompleteness. He had begun to sweat cold, apprehensive drops. "We really are tangled up with something, then."

"Don't start imagining all that old scare stuff," Nina said sharply. "Invasion of Earth—beings from outer space. They're just not that way. They're plants; all they care about is protecting themselves. All they want to do is neutralize us—and that's what they've done." Helplessly, she spread her hands. "It's already happened! It's over! We have our little area to operate in, about six star systems. And then—" She smiled frigidly. "Beyond that, the ring."

"And Jones didn't know?"

"When he started, no. He's known for a year, but what could he do? The war had begun . . . by the time he found out it was too late. He gambled and lost."

"But he didn't admit he was gambling. He said he *knew*."

"That's right: he lied. He could see a lot of things, but he couldn't see everything. So now he's paying for it . . . he's letting the fleet come back. He led us—he led the people—into a trap. He let us down; betrayed us."

"What next?"

"Next," Nina said, pale and subdued, "he puts up his real fight. This afternoon he called all of us together, all the officials of the organization." She unbuttoned her gray coat and showed him the inside lapel. An elaborate emblem-badge was stitched into the fabric, a series of letters and numbers beneath a stylized ornament. "I'm a big shot, darling. I'm vice commissioner of the Women's Defense League . . . part of the new internal security system. So I was herded in with the other very-important-people, stood up in a long row, and fed the real story, our first preview of what's coming."

"How's he taking it?"

"He's almost out of his mind."

"Why?"

"Because," Nina answered, sipping her coffee, "even with his power, *he's still lost.* He can see defeat and death . . . he can see his awful, final struggle to keep alive—and he can see it failing. There it was, on his face. That terrible cadaverous look, like a dead thing. Fish eyes. No life, no luster. He stood there shaking all over; he could scarcely stand up. He twitched, he stammered . . . it was heartbreaking. And he told us the Crusade had failed, was coming back, that in a short while we could expect the riots to break out."

Cussick pondered. "The riots. The betrayed followers."

"Everybody. Except the skeleton of the organization, the real fanatics. They'll fight like hell for him."

"Are there many of them?"

"No, not many. Idealists, the energetic youth. After all, Jones did let us down—it's a fact, he knows it, we know it, pretty soon everybody will know it. But there are those who will stick with him anyhow." Without emotion she added, "Not me."

"Why not?"

"Because," she said slowly, softly, "he told us what he's going to do to keep power. He's going to use the fleet as a weapon against the mobs. He's going to give the fleet its battle. And that means—" Her voice faltered, broke, then resumed. "Well, that means civil war. Just because he lied

to us and betrayed us and led us into ruin we'll never get out
of, doesn't mean he's going to step down; as a matter of fact
he's just getting started. If anybody thinks—"

Cussick reached out and caught hold of her arm. "Take it
easy," he told her firmly. "Lower your voice."

"Thanks." She nodded tightly. "It's so damn awful. He
knows he can't do it—he knows they'll get to him, eventually.
Six months; that's how much time he has. But he's going to
hang on. He's going to pull the whole world down around
his ears . . . if he's dead he wants everybody else dead, too."

Silence.

"And," Nina finished wanly, "there's nothing we can do.
Remember the assassin? Remember Pearson's attempt? It
slipped right into Jones' hands . . . it got him into power."

"What happened to Pearson?"

"Pearson is dying. Very slowly and carefully. Not long ago
Jones introduced some kind of parasite into him. It's feeding
on him; eventually it'll lay its eggs in him. Jones is so proud
of it; he never gets tired telling us about it."

Licking his dry lips, Cussick said hoarsely: "That's the kind
of man you've been following?"

"We had a dream," Nina said simply. "And he had a
dream. It went sour, it went all to pieces . . . but he just
won't let go. He won't stop. And there's nothing that can
make him stop; all we can do is sit back and watch while he
goes to work. The round-ups are beginning. Everybody connected with Fedgov will be destroyed. Then—very rationally
and systematically—every group even remotely capable of
opposition will be smashed."

Cussick's fingers tore up his paper napkin and shredded
the bits onto the floor. "Does Jones know you've crossed
back?"

"I don't think so. Not yet."

"I thought he knew everything."

"He knows only what he's *going* to know. He may never find out; after all, I'm only one of many: he's got millions of people to keep tabs on. A lot of us sneaked off; the man who drove me was my boss, my superior. He was leaving, too, with his wife and family. They're pulling out in droves, trying to find places to hide. Setting up retreats, hoping to last it out."

"I want you to go back," Cussick said.

Nina gave a little soundless bleat. "*Back?*" Quavering, she asked: "You're going to try to talk to him? Reason with him?"

"No," Cussick answered. "Not exactly."

"Oh." Nina nodded, understanding. "I see."

"Probably I'm doing what Pearson did; the quixotic gesture has already been made once. But I can't sit here." He leaned toward her. "Can *you?* Can you sit here sipping your coffee while he gets this thing going?"

Nina couldn't meet his gaze. "All I want to do is get out of it. I want to be back with you." Her eyes on her coffee cup, fingers clutching convulsively, she hurried on: "I have a place. It's in West Africa, where there's still a lot of un-claimed land. I fixed it up months ago; everything's arranged. The place was built by organization labor gangs; it's all fin-ished. I have Jackie down there now."

"That's not legal. It takes both of us."

"There's no such thing as not legal, anymore. Don't you know that? It's what we want—it's what the organization orders. I've got it arranged; we can get down there by to-morrow morning if we leave now. An organization intercon ship will fly us to Léopoldville. From there we'll go by surface car, up into the mountains."

"Sounds fine," Cussick commented. "Sounds like we could get by. We might even be alive, six months from now."

"I'm sure of it," Nina said emphatically. "Look at those Venusians—he doesn't care about them. A lot of people are going to survive; he'll have his hands full coping with the big-city riots."

Cussick examined his wristwatch. "I want you to go back to your organization and I want you to take me along. Can you get me through the check system?"

"If we go back," Nina said evenly, her voice low and steady, "we'll never get out. I know it—I can feel it. We won't get away."

After a moment Cussick said: "One of the things Jones taught us is the importance of action. I think the time for action has come. Maybe I should have been a Jones supporter. This is the time for me to show up and volunteer as one of the Jones Boys."

Nina's trembling fingers slipped from her cup; the cup turned on its side and oozed lukewarm coffee across the table in an ugly brown film. Neither of them moved, neither of them noticed.

"Well?" Cussick inquired.

"I guess," Nina said faintly, "you don't really care about me after all. You don't really want me back."

Cussick didn't answer. He sat waiting for her to agree, to begin putting the wheels into motion that would carry him inside the Jones organization and to Jones himself. And he was wondering, idly at first and then with growing hopelessness, how he could possibly kill a man who knew the topography of the future. A man who could not be taken unawares: a man for whom surprise was impossible.

"All right," Nina said, in an almost inaudible voice.

"Can you get an organization car?"

"Sure." Listlessly, she rose to her feet. "I'll go phone. He can pick us up here."

"Fine," Cussick said, with satisfaction. "We'll wait."

18

Dark rain swished down on the car as the gray-uniformed organization driver guided it conscientiously along through the heavy, slow-moving traffic. In the back, Nina and Cussick sat silently together, neither of them speaking.

Outside the car, blinding headlights loomed up, reflected from a billion raindrops streaking the plastic windows. Signal lights blinked on and off; within the dashboard, answering relays closed in response. The driver had little to do beyond steering; most of the controls were automatic circuits. He was young and blond, a humorless functionary, performing his job skillfully, dispassionately.

"Hear the rain," Nina murmured.

The car halted for a series of rerouting lights. Cussick began shifting restlessly. He lit a cigarette, stubbed it out, then jerkily lit another. Presently Nina reached out and took hold of his hand.

"Darling," she said wretchedly. "I wish—what the hell can I do? I wish I could do something."

"Just get me in."

"But how are you going to do it? It isn't possible."

Warningly, Cussick indicated the driver. "Let's not talk about it."

"He's all right," Nina said. "He's part of my staff."

The car started up, and in a moment they were on the broad freeway that led directly to the Fedgov buildings, where Jones had entrenched himself. It wouldn't be long, Cussick realized. Probably another half hour. Glumly, he gazed out at the lines of speeding cars. There was a lot of traffic. Along the pedestrian ramps shuffled hunched-over citizens, commuters who had been deposited by the urban expresses, dumped off to shift for themselves in the pouring rain.

From his pocket, he got out a small glittering bauble, carefully wrapped in transluscent brown fiber. He sat with his knees apart, holding the bauble cupped in his hands.

"What is it?" Nina asked. Pathetically, she reached out to touch it. "A present for me?"

"We used these all the time," Cussick said, blocking her fingers. "Until Pearson ruled against them. You've probably heard about them . . . the Communists developed them during the war as instruments for conversion. We picked the idea up, too. This is called a lethe-mirror."

"Oh," Nina said. "Yes." She nodded. "I've heard of them. But I didn't think there were any left."

"Everybody kept one or two." In Cussick's hands the bauble shimmered menacingly. All he had to do was remove the brown-fiber covering; it was as simple as that. The mirror was a focus that caught and trapped the attention of the higher brain centers.

The car slowed a trifle. "Are we there?" Cussick demanded instantly.

"No sir," the young driver answered. "There's some kids trying to hitch a ride. Want me to pick them up?" He added, "It's raining pretty hard."

"Sure," Cussick said. "Pick them up."

The four kids who tumbled gratefully into the car were loaded down with drenched wicker baskets and the sodden remains of pennants. "Thanks," the leader gasped, a girl in her middle teens. "You saved our lives."

"We were out selling Crusade buttons," another girl explained, mopping rainwater from her face. Wet brown hair plastered over her ears, she hurried on joyfully: "And we had sold almost all of them, too, before the rain started."

The third teen-ager, a plump red-faced boy, gazed in awe at Nina and squeaked: "Are you in the organization?"

"That's right," Nina said thinly.

The girls mopped at their drenched clothes, struggled to dry their hair, exuded the smell of wet fabric and excitement. "Say," one of them noticed, "this is an official car."

The first girl, small and sharp-faced, with large interested eyes, said shyly to Cussick: "Do you have a Crusade button?"

"No," Cussick answered shortly. The irony of it hit home: this was a typical group of young fanatics, peddling buttons to raise Crusade funds. Standing on street corners, stopping cars and pedestrians, shoppers and commuters, faces flushed and alive with the fervor of their cause. In the four young faces he saw nothing but innocent excitement; for them, the Crusade was a great and noble thing; a spiritual salvation.

"Would you—" the little sharp-faced girl began, glancing up at him timidly, "would you like to buy a Crusade button?"

"Sure," Cussick said. "Why not?" He dug into his pocket. "How much?"

Nina made a strangled sound and ducked her head; he ignored her as he fished out a few crumpled bills.

"Ten dollars is the usual," the girl said, reaching quickly into her wicker basket for a button. "Anything you want . . . it's for a good cause."

He gave her the money; gravely, hesitantly, she pinned the button on his coat. There it hung, a small shield of bright plastic, with the raised sword of the Crusade superimposed on the familiar crossed-flasks. It gave him an unhappy and intricate feeling to sense it there. Suddenly he reached for-ward and lifted a second button from the wicker basket.

"Here," he said gently to Nina. "For you."

Solemnly, he pinned it on her coat. Nina smiled faintly and reached out to touch his hand.

"Now we all have one," the sharp-faced girl said shyly.

Cussick paid her for the second button, and she scrupu-lously put the money with the other contributions. The six people in the back seat rode on through the rain, silent and subdued, each deep in his own thoughts. Cussick wondered what the four kids would be doing and thinking in a few more days. God knew . . . God and Jones, the two of them knew. *He* certainly didn't.

The driver let off the kids at a central intersection; the doors slammed after them, they waved thankfully, and again the car picked up speed. Ahead lay the ominous gray square that was the reinforced, bomb-proof Fedgov buildings. They were almost there.

"Those kids," Nina said sadly. "That's the way I felt, not so long ago."

"I know," Cussick answered.

"They don't mean any harm. They just don't understand."

He leaned down and kissed her; her moist, warm lips clung futilely to his own until, regretfully, he pulled away. "Wish me luck," he told her shortly.

"I do." She clutched fervently at him. "Please try not to let anything happen to you."

Cussick touched his coat. Inside, in addition to the mirror, was a standard police pistol. The mirror was for Jones; the pistol was to get himself back out again, past the guards. "How far inside can you get me?" he asked her. "How high does your authority go?"

"All the way," she answered, face stark-white, breath com-ing in rapid gasps. "It won't be hard . . . they all know me."

"Here we are, sir," the driver said. The car had left the freeway; now it was descending a long ramp toward the garages of the building. An echoing rumble rose around them; the wheels of the car were gliding over steel runners. In the gloom, lights flashed on and off; the car responded instantly. It slowed almost to a halt as the driver turned it over to the garage control. Moving at a snail's pace, it gradually came to a halt. The motor clicked off, and the brake spiraled itself into lock-position. They had arrived.

Warily, Cussick opened the door and stepped out. He recognized this chamber; the vast concrete cave, in the old days, had housed his car. A gray-uniformed attendant was walking over: that was the only difference. The man wore an organization uniform, instead of the police brown. He touched his cap respectfully. "Evening," he murmured. "Can I have your permit?"

"I'll talk to him," Nina said, slipping quickly from the car and hurrying over beside Cussick. She fumbled in her purse and got out the metal plate. "Here it is; the car's mine."

"When did you want to pick it up?" the attendant asked, examining the plate and then returning it to Nina. The first hurdle, at least, was over. "You want it stored overnight?"

"Keep it up on the ground level," Nina instructed, with a questioning glance at Cussick. "We may need it any time."

"Yes ma'am," the attendant agreed, again touching his cap. "It'll be waiting for you."

As they entered the elevator, Cussick's legs were weak. Nina was terribly pale; he took hold of her and dug his fingers into her arm until she winced.

"I'm all right," she said brightly.

"Is it always this busy?" They were crushed in with a tightly-packed group of earnest-faced officials.

"Not always. There's been so much, lately . . ." Her voice trailed off vaguely. "A lot of activity."

The elevator closed at that moment: they stopped talking,

gritted their teeth and hung on to consciousness. Officials were muttering out floor numbers; Nina pulled herself together and said: "Seventeen, please."

They emerged with a knot of fast-moving dignitaries who hurried off in various directions. Ahead loomed the reception lounge and the broad information desk. Nina advanced toward the desk, her heels clicking on the hard, polished floor.

"I'd like an appointment with Mr. Jones," she said huskily to the uniformed officials behind the desk. From her purse she got out all her identification papers and laid them on the surface of the desk. "It's for this man."

Leisurely, the official picked up her papers and studied them. He was middle-aged, with a bulging neck that hung in wattles over his tight collar. His fingers were plump, white, efficient. With petulant, bureaucratic interest, he examined each paper before he spoke. "What's the reason for your request? You'll have to go through the regular channels, Miss Longstren. We have appointments booked up for the next twelve hours." Reluctantly, he got out his book and ran a finger down the column. "It might not be until tomorrow morning."

Nina shot a mute, agonized look at Cussick. "This is an emergency," she faltered. "It should be put right through."

"Well, then," the official said, without particular interest, "you'll have to fill out a special declaration." From a drawer he took a form-pad and turned it toward her. "Indicate the particulars in section five and again in section eight. Make certain the carbons are in properly." He pointed to a small table in the corner of the lounge. "You can fill it out over there."

Numbly, Nina and Cussick carried the pad to the table and seated themselves. "Well?" Nina demanded, in a stricken voice. "What'll I say?"

"Say you're with somebody from the astronomical research

labs. Say there've been some clues on the nature of the ring around us."

Dutifully, Nina filled out the form. "See those men waiting over there? They're waiting to see him . . . and they're all big shots. He's been in conference for a week straight."

She signed the form, and the two of them walked slowly back to the desk. A line had formed; when their turn finally came, the official brusquely accepted the form, scanned it, tore it from the pad, and dropped it into the recording slot. "Please be seated," he told them fussily. "It'll be a half-hour at the very least before Mr. Jones has time to examine your request." He added: "Help yourselves to magazines."

They found seats. Bolt upright, the two of them waited, magazines clutched listlessly. Officials moved back and forth everywhere; from the side corridors came the sound of voices, the muted clank of equipment. The building hummed with restless activity.

"They're busy," Cussick commented. He thumbed through a copy of the *Saturday Evening Post,* and then restored it to the rack.

Nina nodded, too frightened to speak. Eyes fixed on the floor, she sat rigidly clutching her purse and magazine, lips a thin bloodless line. Cussick reached into his pocket until his fingers touched the lethe-mirror. Stealthily, he unwrapped it. Now it was operative . . . all he had to do was draw it out.

But he didn't really believe he had a chance.

"Are you sorry?" Nina asked faintly. "Wish you hadn't come?"

"No," he answered. "I'm not sorry."

"It isn't too late . . . we could just get up and leave."

He didn't answer. He was afraid to; it wouldn't take much more, only the merest pressure, to lift him to his feet and carry him out of the building. A house with Nina and Jackie. The three of them together again, as they had been . . . he turned his mind from the thought and contemplated the dour information clerk, processing forms.

The clerk nodded to him. Stiffly, unbelievingly, Cussick got up and walked over. "Us?" he inquired hoarsely.

"You can go on in."

Cussick blinked. "You mean it's cleared?"

"Mr. Jones accepted it immediately." Without looking up from his work, the clerk nodded toward a side door. "In there, and please complete your business as quickly as possible. Others are waiting."

Cussick walked back to Nina; she watched him, wide-eyed, all the way across the lounge. "I'm going in," he told her briefly. "It might be better if you left. As long as I've gotten through, there's no need of your staying here."

Quietly, she got to her feet. "Where should I go?"

"Back to the apartment. Wait for me there."

"All right," she agreed. She didn't say anything more; without a word, she turned and walked quickly from the lounge, back the way they had come, to the elevator.

As Cussick approached the inner office, he wondered grimly why the application had so readily been accepted. He was still mulling it over when four gray-uniformed workers rose up and confronted him. "Papers," one of them said, hand out. "Your papers, mister."

Cussick passed over the material the information clerk had returned to him; the workers examined it, examined him, and were satisfied. "Good enough," one said. "Go ahead."

A triple, interlocked section rolled noisily back, and Cussick found himself facing more offices and corridors. There were fewer people, here; his footsteps echoed in the dismal silence. For a time he walked along a wide carpeted hallway; nobody was in sight; nobody met him. An almost religious quiet hung over the corridor . . . there were no ornaments, no pictures or statues or bric-a-brac, only the carpet, the sheer walls, the ceiling. At the far end of the hall was a half-closed door. He reached it and halted uncertainly.

"Who's out there?" a voice demanded, a thin, metallic voice, heavy with fatigue, aggravated and querulous. For a moment he didn't recognize it; then identification came.

"Come in," the voice ordered irritably. "Don't stand out there in the hall."

He entered, his hand around the lethe-mirror. Behind a vast littered desk sat Jones, his face wrinkled with weariness and despair. The piled-up work virtually hid him from sight; a tired, defeated puppet struggling with a mountain far too large to be lifted.

"Hello, Cussick," Jones muttered, glancing up briefly. He reached out his claw-like hands and shoved aside some of the heaps of tapes and papers that covered his desk. Squinting nearsightedly, he waved at a chair. "Sit down."

Stunned, Cussick advanced toward the desk. Jones had expected him. Of course . . . he had hidden the obvious from himself. Long before he had seen the application—long before Cussick had dictated it—Jones had know who the "expert from astronomical research" was.

Behind Jones stood two giant, dull-faced, uniformed toughs, gripping machine guns, eyes blank and impassive—as silent and unmoving as statues. Cussick hesitated, fingered the lethe-mirror, started to hold it out.

"Come on," Jones snapped testily, extending his hand. In a single second he had seized the lethe-mirror; without even glancing at it he dropped it to the carpet and ground it to splinters under his heel. Folding his hands together in the center of the desk, he peered up at Cussick. "Will you sit down?" he grated. "I hate to look up. Sit down so we can talk." He groped around among the litter on his desk. "You smoke, don't you? I don't have any cigarettes here; I gave up smoking. It's unhealthy."

"I have my own," Cussick said, reaching unsteadily into his coat.

Fingers drumming restlessly on the desk, Jones said: "I haven't seen you in years, not since that day in the police offices. Work, decrees and whatnot all the time. It's a big job, this type of work. A lot of responsibility."

"Yes," Cussick agreed thickly.

"Pearson is dead, you know. Died this morning." A grotesque leer touched the withered face. "I kept him alive for awhile. He planned my murder, but I was waiting—a whole year ahead of time. Waiting for that assassin to show up. You picked a good time to come; I was just about to send for you. Not just you, of course; everybody in your class, the whole lot of you. And that stupid blonde who used to be your wife; you knew she joined us, didn't you? Of course you knew . . . she filled out this application. I recognize her chicken-tracks."

"Yes," Cussick repeated.

"A lot of sex-starved society females have come to us," Jones rambled on, face twitching, thin body quivering with nervous spasms. His voice was monotonous; the words ran together in a mumbled blur of fatigue. "A sort of substitute for adequate copulation, I suppose . . . this is the lifelong orgasm for them. Sometimes with tricks like your wife around, I get the feeling I'm running a cat house instead of a—"

From his coat, Cussick's hand brought out the gun. He was conscious of no decision; his hand moved on its own volition. In an instinctive, reflexive blur, he aimed and fired.

It was at the larger of the two bodyguards that he had aimed; in some dim way he had the idea that it was necessary to kill them first. But Jones, seeing the glint of metal, had suddenly jumped to his feet. Like a skinny, animated doll, he bounced between Cussick and the two guards; the explosive shell caught him directly above the right eye.

The two guards, paralyzed with disbelief, stood rooted to the spot, without even lifting their guns.

Cussick, too, was unable to stir. He stood holding the pistol, not firing at the guards, not being fired at in return. The body of Jones lay strewn across the littered desk.

Jones was dead. He had killed him; it was over.

It was impossible.

19

When he pushed open the apartment door, Nina gave a shriek and ran sobbing to him. Cussick caught hold of her and held her tight, his mind still swirling aimlessly.

"I'm okay," he muttered. "He's dead. It's over."

She backed away, face streaked with tears, eyes red and swimming. "You killed him?" There was only disbelief there, without comprehension. He felt the same way; her expression mirrored his own. "But *how?*"

"I shot him." He was still holding the pistol. They had let him walk out of the building; nobody had tried to stop him. Nobody comprehended what had happened . . . he had met only dazed shock, comatose figures, stricken and lifeless.

"But you couldn't have killed him," Nina repeated. "Didn't he expect it?"

"I wasn't shooting at him. He was sitting down—I shot at one of the guards." Cussick rubbed his forehead uncertainly. "It was instinctive. He was talking about you . . . I yanked out the gun and fired. Maybe that was it; I didn't plan to. Maybe I changed time. Maybe I somehow altered the future by acting reflexively. Maybe subrational responses can't be predicted."

Clutching at straws, he almost believed it. Almost, he had constructed a convincing rationalization. Almost, he was prepared to accept it—until he saw the small brown package on the arm of the couch.

"What's that?" he demanded.

"This?" Nina picked it up. "I haven't any idea—it came before I got here. From the organization." She held it out. "It's addressed to you. It was lying in the hall, propped against the door."

Cussick took it. The shape of the box was familiar: it was a reel of audtape. With numb fingers he tore off the paper and carried the tape to the playback equipment mounted in the wall above the coffee table.

The voice didn't surprise him. By now the pieces were falling together.

"Cussick," the thin, harried snarl began, "you had better lay low for awhile. There'll probably be a lot of commotion. I don't know; I'm just guessing. You understand? *I'm just guessing.* As far as you're concerned, I've lost my ability, and you realize why."

Yes, he realized why. Jones had seen everything up until the moment of his death. But that was all: nothing beyond that.

"You did a good clean job," Jones' voice continued, the harsh, metallic mutter that he had heard not half an hour ago. "Of course, you shouldn't get the credit. All you did was shoot off that gun; it was up to me to get in its way. But you did what you had to do. That was good; I knew you would. You didn't chicken out."

Cussick halted the tape. "Foxy dried-up little coot," he said savagely.

"Don't stop it!" Nina quavered; snatching his hand away, she clicked the tape-transport mechanism back into motion. "So now," Jones stated, "I'm dead. I can't tell exactly when this will reach you, but I suppose it will. What I do know is this: *if* and when you hear this, I'll be dead, because I've seen that much happen. And by now you've seen it happen, too. Do you grasp how I feel? For one year I've sat facing that moment, knowing it was coming. Knowing it couldn't be avoided. Suffering through that—and through what comes afterward. Now it's over. Now I can rest. You realize, of course, that what you did was what I wanted you to do. But probably you don't understand why.

"I made a mistake. I gambled, I took a chance, and I lost. I was wrong . . . but not in the way you think. I was more wrong than you think."

"No," Cussick said, baffled fury choking up inside him.

"In the next day or so," Jones continued, "the warships will be back home. People would see I made a mistake— they'd realize that I was fallible like everybody else. *They would know I didn't have absolute knowledge.*" An amused mutter of triumph burst through the words, interrupting the monotonous flow. "Pretty soon the word would have started getting around: Jones was a fraud. Jones didn't have any talent. Jones played us for a sucker; he didn't have any more idea of the future than we did. But now they won't think that. They'll have this fact: today, Jones was murdered. And tomorrow, the ships start leaking back in. Jones died before defeat began—and cause always comes first."

Futilely, Cussick slammed off the flow of words. "Christ," he said bitterly.

"I don't get it," Nina whispered, stricken. "What's he mean?"

Reluctantly, Cussick again started up the tape.

"They'll say I was viciously killed," Jones observed glee-fully. "They'll say you stole victory away from them when you murdered me. The legend will grow up: if Jones had lived, we would have won. It was you, the old system, Fedgov, Relativism, that robbed us. *Jones didn't fail.*

"My apologies to your wife. I had to say that; I had to

goad you. Pearson, of course, is alive. You'll find him in one
of the old police prisons; that is, if you're still—"

"You can turn it off," Nina said. "I don't have to hear any
more."

He did so, instantly. "I helped him get what he wanted.
He used me the way he used Pearson . . . we were elements
of his plan."

For a time neither of them spoke.

"Well," Nina said bravely, "we don't have the civil war,
now."

"No," Cussick agreed. "That was all a fake, a plant; all
that stuff he told you about a last ditch stand against the
mobs—that was for my benefit."

"He was quite a psychologist."

"He was everything. He understood history—he knew
when to get off the stage . . . and how. He knew when to
make his entrance and his exit. We thought we were going
to be stuck with Jones for another six months . . . instead,
we're stuck with Jones, the legend of Jones, forever."

He didn't need Jones' talent to see it. The new religion.
The crucified god, slain for the glory of man. Certain to
reappear, someday; a death not in vain. Temples, myths,
sacred texts. Relativism wasn't coming back in, not in this
world. Not after this.

"He really has us," Cussick admitted, furious, baffled, but
forced to admire the cunning of the man. "He outsmarted
us, all the way along the line. There'll be icons of Jones sixty
feet high. He'll grow taller every year—in a century he'll be
a couple of miles high." He laughed harshly. "Shrines. Holy
images."

Nina began rewinding the tape. "Maybe we can use this
as evidence."

"Hell," Cussick told her, "we've got plenty of evidence.
We can *prove* Jones was wrong—prove it a million different

ways. He misjudged the drifters—that's a fact. The ring was up before Jones died; the ships had already started back. And he's dead—rationally, that ought to cinch it. But it won't. He's right; he's a shrewd judge of us. Cause precedes effect. Jones died on Monday, the war was lost on Tuesday. Even I, standing here in this room, can't help being just a little convinced."

"Me too," Nina agreed in a wretched, tiny voice. "It just sort of—*feels* right."

Cussick wandered over to the window, pushed aside the drapes, and gazed out helplessly at the dark sheets of rain drumming on the pavement below.

"What about you and me?" Nina asked timidly. "I guess you don't want to go to West Africa."

"You think West Africa will be far enough away? For *me?* I'm the man who murdered Jones—remember? A lot of people are going to be out looking for me."

"But where can we go?" Nina asked.

"Off Earth," Cussick said, brooding. "There's nowhere here for us. It'll take a day or so for them to start moving . . . that'll barely give us time to get Jackie and the rest of what we need. Junk—tons of it. And a good ship, one that's been recently serviced. You still have enough money and pull for such things?"

She nodded slowly. "Yes, I suppose. You sound like you've made up your mind. You've decided where we're going."

"Where we're going and what we're going to do. It isn't pleasant, but maybe it wouldn't be permanent. That's one consolation . . . this stuff may die down someday, and we can come back."

"I doubt it," Nina said.

"I doubt it, too. But we'll need something to keep us going. We're going to have a few rough times ahead." He turned away from the window. "You can stay here, you realize.

You're legally not my wife; they won't necessarily connect the two of us. A little fast talking here and there, and you're a loyal organization worker again."

"I'll come along," Nina said.

"You're sure? After all, you're in on the ground floor . . . you can be a saint in the new church."

She smiled up sadly. "You know I want to come along. So let's stop stalling around."

"Good," Cussick agreed, a little happier. In fact, a lot happier. Bending, he kissed her on the nose. "You're right— let's get started. The sooner we get out of here, the better."

20

The interior of the cabin was cool and dark. The air, moist with the swirling mist from outside, drifted up in Louis' face and momentarily cut off his view. He blinked, squinted, settled down on his haunches, and leaned closer to see.

"Be careful," Dieter warned him ominously.

In the shadows lay Vivian, covered to her chin by a blanket. She gazed up weakly at Louis, her eyes dark and immense. It gave him a strange feeling; his heart turned over, and he had trouble getting his breath.

"Maybe I better look later," he muttered.

"I don't drive you fifty miles for nothing," Dieter answered urgently. "What's the matter? Afraid?"

"Yes," Louis admitted. "Do I have to look?" Fear took over, and he backed hurriedly away from the bed. What if it wasn't right? There was always the chance, a high chance, a better than even chance. The problem had never been solved; maybe the genes were inviolate, as Mendel had said. But how, then, had evolution occurred? A vast torrent of abstract theory swept through his brain. "No," he said emphatically, "I can't look."

Dieter strode over beside his wife. "You'll be next," he

said to Louis. "You and Irma. And then Frank and Syd. So *look*."

He looked. And it was all right.

Trembling he bent down. The baby was sound asleep, a reddish, healthy face, eyes shut tight, mouth slack, forehead pulled into a rubbery scowl. Tiny arms stuck up, ending in bent fingers. In many ways, it looked like an Earth baby . . . but it wasn't. He could see that already.

The nostrils were altered; he noticed that first of all. A spongy element closed each one: filter-membrane to screen out the thick water vapor. And the hands. Reaching cautiously down, he took hold of the baby's tiny right hand and examined it. The fingers were webbed. No toes at all. And the chest was immense: huge lungs, to gather in enough of the air to keep the fragile organism alive.

And that was the proof. That was the important thing, the real thing. *The baby was alive.* Breathing the Venusian air, withstanding the temperature, the humidity . . . all that remained was the problem of nutrition.

Fondly, Vivian drew the baby against her body. The baby stirred, struggled fitfully, opened its eyes. "What do you think of him?" Vivian asked.

"He fine," Louis said. "What's his name?"

"Jimmy." Vivian smiled up blissfully. Presently she lifted the struggling baby up against her enlarged breasts; after a short while the struggles ceased, and the frantic motion died into a greedy half-doze. Louis watched for a moment, and then he tiptoed off, to where Dieter stood proudly waiting.

"Well?" Dieter demanded belligerently.

Louis shrugged. "It's a baby. It kicks."

The youth's face flushed scarlet. "Don't you understand? It's altered—it's adapted. It'll live."

"Sure," Louis agreed. Then he grinned and slapped the boy on the back. "You're a father, you squirt. How the hell old are you?"

"Eighteen."

"How old is Viv?"

"Seventeen."

"You old patriarch. By the time you're my age, you'll have grandchildren. Virility, thy name is youth."

Frank and Syd came rapidly into the cabin, followed by Laura: now three years old and skipping about ably. Irma appeared behind them, face anxious. "Is it—" she began, and then became quiet and subdued as she made out the two figures in the bed.

"Gosh," Frank said, awed. "It's real."

"Of course it's real!" Dieter shouted.

Garry appeared in the doorway. "Can I come in?"

"Come on in," Louis said. "We're going to have a party." He led Laura over to the bed. "You, too. Everybody can look."

Bending over the woman and her baby, Syd said thoughtfully: "The nutrition problem is solved right now. But what about later?"

"Don't worry about it," Dieter said haughtily. With a little embarrassment he explained: "Rafferty didn't overlook anything. Viv's glands . . . that is . . . the mammary secretions aren't the same. Louis and I made tests. It's milk, but it's not regular milk."

"Thank God," Syd said, relieved.

"I wouldn't want to have to keep him alive for the rest of his life," Vivian said softly. "I don't think I could."

Frank and Louis walked off to confer in private. "This is the best thing that's happened," Frank said. "Have you considered the alternative? Suppose the baby had been normal— an Earth baby, geared to an Earth environment. Suppose all our progeny reverted. Yes, that's the term. Reversion. Suppose we hadn't been able to pass this on? Suppose we were sports, not true mutants?"

"Well, we're not."

"Thank God for that. The eight of us would have lived out our little life-spans and then died. That would have been the end of the race. Some race."

They stepped out of the cool darkness, down the three steps, onto the walk that Dieter had laboriously erected to the main road. In the last year the colony had expanded geometrically. Smooth-surfaced roads linked each of the individual settlements with the others. In front of Dieter's cabin stood a crude metal vehicle he and Garry had built: metal hammered from sheets rolled in their own furnace. It was a grotesque-looking object, but it served its purpose. The vehicle was powered by a storage battery. Its tires were amateurishly molded, not precisely round, but serviceable. The material was a poured plastic, a sap derived from a fern-like tree. The vehicle, on level ground, did ten miles an hour.

"Don't look at it too hard," Louis commented. "It'll collapse."

And that wasn't all. The bubbling fonts of hot water that spilled to the surface were natural sources of electric power. Four generating plants had already been assembled; the new Venusian society had a constant source of heat, light, and general power. Most of the equipment had been removed from the ruined ships and scout domes; but gradually, bit by bit, hand-made elements were being substituted.

"Looks good," Louis admitted.

"It does," Frank agreed. "He's done a lot here. But all those silly-looking animals he's got tied up . . . what the hell are they for?"

"God knows," Louis said. He leaned into the cabin and said to Dieter: "What are those things standing around out here?"

Loftily, Dieter answered: "That's my herd of wuzzles."

"What are they for? You going to eat them?"

With dignity, Dieter explained: "The wuzzle was the dominant species. Intellectually, it's the mose advanced indigenous life-form. Tests I've conducted show the wuzzle is more intelligent than the Terran horse, pig, dog, cat, and crow put together."

"Heavens," Irma murmured.

"They're going to be our helpers," Dieter revealed sleekly. "I'm teaching that particular herd to perform routine chores. So our minds will be free for constructive planning."

Shaking his head, Louis backed out of the cabin.

But it was a good sight. All of it: the fields, the animal sheds, the smoke-house, the silo, the main cabin, now a double-walled building with two bedrooms, a living room, kitchen, and indoor bathroom. And already, Garry had located a substitute for wood-pulp; an abortive paper had been turned out, followed by primitive type. It was only a question of time before their society became a civilization: a civilization, now, of *nine* individuals.

An hour later, Frank and Syd were riding slowly back to their own settlement, in their electric-driven wagon. "It's good news," Frank reiterated, as the countryside crept past on each side of them.

"You said that five times already," Syd pointed out gently.

"It's true, though." Frank meditated, a worried frown on his face. "Maybe we should stop by one of the ships."

"Why?"

"We ought to build an incubator. Suppose the baby had *almost* adapted, but not quite? It might have died . . . but in an incubator, we could keep it alive until it got stronger. Adjust conditions until it could tolerate this environment. Just to be on the safe side." He added plaintively, "I don't want anything to happen to ours."

"We should drop by the domes, at least," Syd said. "They'd like to hear."

Frank turned the wagon from the road; in a moment it was bumping over the knobby greenish slush that made up the Venusian countryside. Ahead of them lay a long line of hazy mountains. At the base was the strewn debris that had once been the Terran protective domes. The war-projectiles had burst them, of course, but out of the remnants a single structure had been assembled. It was a quasi-dome, a hollow half-sphere anchored at the base of the hills.

"It's weird," Frank commented, "seeing that, there. Like being outside your skin."

"Outside your old skin," Syd corrected.

The Refuge wasn't as large as theirs had been; it was only a city block long and a few hundred feet wide. It had been constructed to keep alive three individuals, not eight. But the principle was the same: inside the transparent bubble lay a different world, with different temperature, atmosphere, humidity, and life-forms.

The three inhabitants had done a good job of fixing up their Refuge. It was like a small section of Earth severed from the original. Even the colors were exact; Frank had to admire their handiwork, their skill in creating this authentic replica. But, then, this was all they had been doing the last year. This was all there was for them to do.

They had scrupulously developed an artificial blue sky, an almost convincing imitation of Earth's blue bowl. Here was a cloud. There was a flock of migratory ducks, permanently glued to the inside of the plastic bubble. The man, Cussick, had brought grass seed with him; the bottom surface was a solid expanse of dark lush green, similar to the outside Venusian flora, but not the same.

No, not the same at all. A subtle color difference, and a great difference in texture. It was a different world transplanted here, in miniature. A fragment. A museum-piece that gave Frank an odd nostalgic feeling as the wagon neared it.

The Earth family had grown themselves shrubs and trees. A maple and a poplar tree waved bravely inside the Refuge.

They had, from the materials available, constructed a model of a Terran house, a small two-bedroom residence. White stucco walls. A red-tile roof. Windows, with curtains behind them. A gravel path. A garage (with nothing inside it but an elaborate workbench). Roses, petunias, and a few fuchsias. The cuttings and seeds had all been brought on the original—and only—trip from Earth: Cussick had anticipated what lay ahead. In the back was a thriving vegetable garden. And the man had even thought to bring four chickens, a cow and a bull, three pigs, a pair of dogs, a pair of domestic cats, and a flock of assorted birds.

The Refuge was literally jammed with Terran flora and fauna. The woman, Nina, had painted an artificial backdrop that was startlingly convincing. Rolling brownish hills, with a distant blue ocean. The woman was quite talented along artistic lines; she had supervised the development of the creation with a trained and critical eye. Playing at the edge of the Refuge, where the backdrop began, was their four-year-old son Jack. He was busily assembling a sand castle at the edge of a small synthetic lake in which lapped painstakingly distilled water.

"I feel sorry for them," Syd said abruptly.

"You do? Why?"

"Because it's awful. You remember . . . Living like that, shut up in a little glass box."

"Someday they'll be able to go back," Frank reminded her. "One of these days the Society of the Prince of Man—or whatever the new hagiocracy is called—will cool off and let him return."

"If he hasn't died of old age."

"They're cooling; it won't be long. And remember: *he knows why he's here*. He decided; it was voluntary. And it has a purpose."

Frank turned off the motor of the wagon and brought it

to a halt. He and Syd stepped gingerly down and walked toward the Refuge. Inside, beyond the transparent wall, Cussick had seen them. He walked toward them, waving.

Cupping his hands to his mouth, Frank shouted: "It's a boy. It's adapted—everything's fine."

"He can't hear you," Syd reminded him gently.

Together, they entered the intermediary lock. There, seated on stools, they clicked on the microphone and warmed up the communication system that linked them to the interior of the Refuge, the finite cosmos beyond. Around them, pipes and circuits wheezed; this was the intricate pumping equipment that kept the atmosphere of the Refuge constant. Beyond that were the thermostatic elements, ripped from the three damaged ships. And beyond that, the most important equipment of all: the manufacturing units that processed the Earthpeople's food.

"Hi," Cussick said, standing beyond the viewing wall, hands in his pockets, a cigarette between his lips. His sleeves were rolled up; he had been working in his garden. "How'd it come out?"

"He came out fine," Syd said.

"Adapted?"

"Totally. A regular monster."

"Fine," Cussick said, nodding. "We'll split a beer on it."

His wife appeared, a plump, pretty figure in blue slacks and halter, a streak of orange paint across her bare stomach, face glistening with perspiration. In one hand she carried a block of sandpaper and a paint scraper. She looked well-fed and content; quite happy, in fact. "Give her our congratulations," Nina's voice came. "It's a boy?"

"Absolutely," Frank said.

"It's healthy?"

"Healthy as a wuzzle," Frank said. "In fact, it's the new wuzzle. The replacement wuzzle, a better wuzzle to take the place of the old."

Puzzled, Nina shook her head. "You're not coming through. Your words are all garbled."

"Don't worry about it," her husband told her, putting his arm around her waist and pulling her to him. "Worry about the mice in the pantry."

"Mice!" Syd exclaimed. "You brought mice along?"

"I wanted things to be natural," Cussick explained, grinning. "I even boxed up some grasshoppers and flies. I want my world to be complete. As long as we have to stay here—"

Over by the synthetic lake, Jackie played happily with his sand castle.

"I want him to know what he's going to be up against," Cussick explained. "So he'll be prepared, when the three of us go back."